Dedicated to those that lost
their lives or their freedom due
to the Game.

Da Brickz: Life in the Game

by

John A Galeotto

Norfolk Publishing Group
Boston, MA

Norfolk Publishing Group

www.npgbooks.com

info@npgbooks.com

Da Brickz: Life in the Game

A Norfolk Publishing Group Book

Publishing History Norfolk Publishing Group eBook
Edition/October 2019
Norfolk Publishing Group trade paperback Edition /May
2015

ISBN-13: 987-1-950-45700-7
ISBN-10: 1-950-45700-1

Book and Cover design by Chris DiRusso
www.chris-dirusso.com

Fan mail: j.galeotto@npgbooks.com
More author info: www.john-a-galeotto

Contents

Chapter Zero

Before anyone could react, Damien walked across the blacktop of the basketball court with burner in hand. He couldn't believe the decision to spark a spliff would be the deciding factor in *ending* some motherfucker's life. *Fuck it*. This cat deserved to die.

He raised his burner as he shouted, "Yo, mutha-fucka!"He paused, as he gritted his teeth."You poor excuse of a fucker mutha-sicka!" Twisting up his words making no sense.

"W-what's the prob?" the man said, backing away…almost stumbling. "Thought we were cool, dawg? What's tha deal, son?"

"Not your son, ya bitch-*ass*-maggot," Damien said, as images from the security footage flooded his head.

"You gots to die. Enough said, muthafucka!" Damien squeezed the trigger of his FN57, sending a 5.7mm armor-piercing bullet hurtling in the plead-ing man's direction, hitting him high on the chest. The blood pooled through his T-shirt in a Rorschach like pattern. Instantly the man collapsed to the asphalt, as another slug plunged through his ribcage.

Pandemonium broke out. People fled for their lives. Only a few people stayed to watch Damien body dude. He glanced around before walking over to the man screaming in agony. Damien could care less about anything else at this point. He was in a killing zone. Nothing else mattered or existed, as he carried out his task. *Nothing*.

He had trouble believing that it had only been five years since he got in the Game. Shit, he never would have thought that he would've taken part in several murders and given orders to many more. Damien was more than a hustler — he was a W8 Mova and sometimes people needed to be eliminated.

Damien was the leader of a well-known crew, but this piece of shit fucked things up on him, by doing what he did. This was more than just business. It became personal. *No justice like street justice.*

Damien raised the burner one more time and squeezed another slug out of the blazing hot barrel, sending the down man's mind into darkness. One doesn't become a body until their dead. Damien turned to leave, calmly walking back to his whip. As he walked, he thought about when he'd first been introduced to the place that would become his home…and lead him to the Game.

Chapter One

Growing up, outside of Boston, in a city rife with violence made Damien cautious, but he still loved runnin them streets.

Everything was out on display no matter where you went in the city. Prostitution down on Union Street, pushers on most corners, and more than three hundred flags down on the commons. Of course, you would see all the bangers in different hoods as well. All at the same time — *it was crazy.*

The you had the Hell's Angels and other Big-boys. Nice bikes and customized whips. He loved the city of Sin. Lynn was more than his home; it was his life. Well, up until he started going to visit his father's house 60 miles away.

That's when his world started to change.

When Damien was in the city, he was smoking weed and doing stupid kid things. The hustlin side of the streets didn't mean too much to him. However, he knew a few hustlers who did their thing. A view that started to change after he went down to stay the summer at his father's in what he believed was a small, sleepy town. American's Hometown: Plymouth.

Damien thought the summer would be the worst one of his life. Instead, it was the one that changed his entire outlook on life and Da Brickz. It's when he discovered Da Brickz were everywhere. Ghettos weren't exclusive to the city — towns had them too and Plymouth was no exception.

By the time Damien was ten-years-old, he was already knee deep in his share of shit. Damien's mother tried her best to raise him and his two older brothers. Most of her time was spent correcting him. His brothers never did much dirt. They concentrated on sports, girls, and school. He wasn't into sports like that, and at ten-years-old he'd rather run the streets a muck with his friends, smoking something and drinking 40's like the older cats around the way.

Damien got into more than his share of trouble. He had a bad temper and fought all the time. Damien would listen to no one. Even this older cat tried to school him. Damien tried his best to listen to him, because the cat was a serious dude. But the dude got caught up on some other shit and was no longer around. *Probably in prison or something.*

Just after he turned twelve, his mother had enough. She found some weed in his pants, and his clothes smelled like he had been swimming in a brewery. She would, usually, call his father and he would go down to his father's house for the week-end as punishment, and catch a hot-one from his dad. A beating if you didn't know.

This time, however, she had other plans — Damien went down for the entire summer. She believed Damien wouldn't get into trouble down there. At least not as much as he could get into up in the city. His mom also thought the cause of his trouble was the city. *Boy, was she wrong.* The cause of Damien's troubles was himself. It was *all* him. He visited his father a few times. The block he lived on was all right.

It really wasn't any different than where he was from: Teenage cats chillin, drinking, even some cats posted up at the corner where he stayed. It was like the city, except contained within a few blocks. There was even a Walmart across the street where his father insisted he buy Damien's clothes.

So now he was out there, straight busted, in a new place. At least, Damien had some friends from his visits on those past weekends. He also hung out with an older cousin. It was peace except for the fact his father hated him being around and told him so. Every day, he would get drunk and talk shit about everything Damien did. Damien made sure he was never home.

The block became his home and his friends his fam. Damien was heavily into partying that went on that summer, along with all the trouble he could find.

Chapter Two

Damien woke up one morning to his pop's shouting, "You little fucking bastard!" He covered his head with is pillow, paying him no mind. "Where the fuck were you last night?"

Damien knew he should've waited until his father went to work instead of coming in at 5:30 in the morning. *Damn, why is he always riding me?*

"Look, you're supposed to be in at ten. *No* later. You better stop disobeying me, Damien," his father said, feeling ignored, before adding, "'cause I'll beat your little fuckin delinquent ass!"

Damien figured he had no choice but to talk to him. *Damn, I hate this shit!*

"Dad leave me alone; I'm trying to sleep."

"Yeah, I'll leave you alone, alright," he said, "when I send you back to your fuckin mother's."

"I'm Sorry," Damien said sheepishly. "I fell asleep over Jimmy's watching a movie."

"I told you, Damien," he said, "I don't want you hanging around those punks."

"They're not punks, dad. They're my friends."

"*Punks!*"

"You can't tell me who I can hang wit."

"I can and just did," his father stated, before turning to leave the room. "I'm going to work. Clean up your room and do the fuckin dishes!" He shouted before the door to the apartment slam shut.

Why is it when parents get mad, they always tell you to clean something: Room, dishes, house.

His head was still spinning and pounding from drinking too much the night before. He also knew his Pop's wasn't done yelling at him. He never was. Plus, when he came home after work, he'd be drunk as usual. Damien would have to avoid him tonight for sure. He didn't feel like getting his ass beat. *Do most kids go through this? Hope not.*

Damien knew Jimmy didn't have to go through this shit. His family was cool. They would rather see him do his thing at home where they could keep an eye on him. Of course, Jimmy still partied on the block.

Damien wondered if he was awake yet.

He wished he had a phone, as he got out of bed and headed for the fridge, while his stomach growled. Shit, he wished he had cable too. It was 2006 not 1980. *Fuck it.* It was August and the summer was off-the-hook, and it wasn't over yet. He never thought it was live — never mind off-the-hook — down here. 'Cause if he knew, he would have come down more often. He opened the fridge. *Damn, nothing to eat, shit! Cereal; no milk. Hot dog rolls; no hot dogs,* he thought shutting the barren fridge. However, his father left three dollars on the kitchen table for him and no note. He must have felt bad for yelling at him.

"What*ever*," he mumbled to himself, as he decided to take a shower, get dressed, and hit the block.

$

There were only a few cats chillin' at the corner. Two of them his boys: Desaun, an older cat that chilled with everyone, and Damien's boy Jimmy. As he crossed the street, Damien shouted: "What up dawg?"

"What up, Kid? Jimmy replied

Then looking at Desaun, "What up?"

"What's going on lil nigga?" Desaun replied.

"Not much at all," Damien said, letting out a sigh, "ya feel me?"

They nodded.

They were posted up on the block for a while, when Desaun decided to take a walk to go get a blunt and said he would catch up with them later. Damien and Jimmy decided to stay back.

"Yo, dawg," Damien said. "My Pop's was flipppin out this morning. He done woke me up yelling' and shit. *Sheesh*!" he said, shaking his head. "Glad he wasn't drunk, dawg, 'cause that would've really sucked."

"Sorry to hear that," Jimmy said. "I'm glad my peeps don't trip like that. Hell, my peeps keep it real, son—"

"I feel ya,"

"—as long as I keep my grades up, they could care less."

"Man, you got any money?" Damien's stomach still growling.

"Yeh, ten bucks, why? What's up?"

"I got three and I'm hungry. Wanna get some grub?"

"Yeh, sure," Jimmy said, standing up.

They left the block to walk to the Kingston House of Pizza, down the street. They got their grub on and then went over to their boy Roc's crib. Damien loved going over to Roc's house because his older sister and her friends were all fine, straight dimes.

Their boy Roc was the only thirteen-year-old pimp Damien knew. This kid was always with some fine chick. Roc may have been only a year older than Damien, but even by the time Damien reached 30, he still would not have slept with as many girls as Roc did then. Not even close. Roc just didn't care who he slept with. He would sleep with anyone. Having a pussy was the only requirement. Damien and Jimmy loved to chill over there, smoking spliffs, and eating all their food.

Desaun came through to holla at Roc's sister and brought a Dutch for them to match. This way there would be two blunts to smoke. After hours of playing video games, while getting blazed the fuck up, and chomping all the munchies in the house, they hit the block again. Jimmy called everyone from Roc's, so they could meet them at the stoop.

When they arrived, the whole gang was already there, along with some older cats who just chilled on the block too. Damien, Jimmy, and Roc met up with: Ty, this athletic looking cat; Dez, the official pothead; Julio, an Italian kid, they would fuck with by calling him Who-lee-o, when it was pronounced Jul-lee-o; Jon Jon, the lazy one of the crew; and then there was Crazy E, they called him that because, well, he was.

The females that were tight with them were also out: Kim, a future dime piece, at least the way Damien saw it; Teri, the most conceited of the girls, who knew she was fine and wouldn't stop telling you; and then there was Tanisha, an older gangsta chick who just chilled on the block every now and again.

This was Damien's block and the people with whom he chilled. Of course, there were others, however, these were the ones he saw on the regular. After they met up, they chilled like every other night, partying out of control.

The night was crazy. The summer was definitely off the hizzie fo' shizzie. Dez brought the green. Haze, some purple. They blazed it in Dutches as well as pipes and bongs…experimenting with all kinds of devices. And there was liquor and beer. Name your favorite, it was there. It turned out that four cats were having a party at the same time, so it was like the Ave was having one giant block party. And you had the dealers pushing their product, hoes giving up the sex, along with dumb motherfuckers causing problems, making the spot hot.

There were people in the streets. Everyone was having a good time. His crew was hanging out in the back of Dave and Melissa's where Ty also lived. They chilled there till they got kicked out, for being too loud.

There were some people chillin in the backyard next store, so they went there where no one would fuck with them. People respected the spot because it belonged to Kain, a cat Damien had never met.

They were having a good time until some cats from another neighborhood came through with some drama. The little sister to one of the cats was hanging out with Damien and them. So, it gave these ignorant cats a reason to be the bitch-ass mother-fuckers everyone knew they were. Jose could have swung through to get his sister, maybe even chilled, but instead he came with an attitude, acting a fool and insulting everyone, on some other shit.

They were foolish to come cause trouble, because there were only four of them and ten times that many hangin out with Damien, if you counted the older cats. That didn't stop Jose. It didn't even slow him down. He grabbed up his sister and bitched her out, for chilling with Damien and his friends.

Jose was straight up disrespectful, he even called her out her name. And to top it off he slapped the dog-shit out of her when she talked back. He was only a year older than her, but despite being seventeen he acted like her father. Jose was a jackass before this and never got invited to party because he was a straight asshole. It was around this time that one of Damien's crew felt disrespected: Crazy E wasted no time smashing a 40oz over Jose's head. Everyone started stomping them for bringing the drama. The chick never chilled with them before and never again. *They weren't about drama.*

The older cats broke it up, reminding everyone who lived there—Kain—and everybody dipped. No one seemed to want to disrespect this cat Kain. It made Damien wonder who he was. It was the last thing Damien could remember.

Crazy things happened on the block: People sold weed, pills, various forms of cocaine. The block was live. The street wasn't called Crack Ave for nothing. Everyone stayed out to one or two in the morning. The older cats who had those parties always invited Damien and his people. The summer was the best one of Damien's young life. He even got laid a few times and being twelve that was a big thing. The summer was going by fast—so was his life. *Maybe a little too fast.*

After another morning of being rudely woken by his father's yelling, his father informed him that he was going home. Why, because Damien, according to him, wasn't listening. But it was okay with Damien. He was sick of the bullshit. Damien's Pops was never happy with him. No matter what he did, it was wrong.

Well, after the last time he got bitched at, Damien had forgotten to clean his room and do the dishes. His father came home and beat the living shit out of him. Bad. *Fuck it.* He was happy to be going home, except he'd miss his friends. Nevertheless, he packed up his stuff, said goodbye to his friends, and went back home. Sin City.

When Damien got back to the city, he was excited at first to see all his friends. Although he found it funny that after only a week, he really missed his father's. More to the truth, his new friends. The block at his father's was more exciting than his up in the city. It just didn't make sense to him that the block was jumping-off down there — and nothing was poppin off up at his mom's. Damien could hardly wait until he could go back to his father's.

Damien started visiting his dad every other weekend for about a year. That is, until his mom got fed up with him skipping school and getting caught with weed and shit. *The last straw*.

She shipped Damien off to his father. This time, however, to live. It was getting close to spring and summer, which was fast approaching. Damien still had time to make a few more friends before school let out.

Chapter Three

Well, the summer came and went. And to Damien, it was as much fun, if not more, than the last. He was coming up to his third summer when he found out that the cat who once tried to school him lived in the building next to the stoop—he was the one everyone respected. A legend of sorts because he was serious dude, known to smash a motherfucker's grill in. Damien already knew the man could fight, because he had seen Kain train and spar at the Taekwondo School up in the city…where Damien went for a short time. His mom thought it would help him, it didn't.

After his cousin told him that the cat who tried to school him and the person everyone respected were the one and the same, Damien became awestruck. Shortly after their discussion, He saw Kain and said, "What's up?" He was surprised Kain had remembered him. Kain, who had been released from prison several months earlier wanted to stay low. So he didn't chill on the block. He had gone to prison for some bullshit that Damien didn't know, or care, about. And to Damien's surprise, Kain hung out with his boy Ty's parents and the couple that let them hangout at their crib from time to time.

Damien would often see Kain kickin it with people in his parking lot, or in his backyard, where he would chill when he was around. Kain was crisp, head to toe—hair boxed-out: a tight fade. Perfect. Kain's clothes were brand new and every day he rocked a different pair of kicks. Damien knew he had money. He also learned that he owned Da Urban Clothing Store up at the mall.

Although it was in the middle of summer when Damien found out that Kain was the *man*: The weed, E, OXYs, and some of the best coke on the street was said to be his. Damien would never have guessed Kain to be a hustler. He didn't think Kain did anything except run his clothing store, which wasn't his only one. He had others. Damien, up until that moment, believed Kain to be legit.

Dave and Melissa sold dimes of weed they got from Kain. One day when Damien was over there, Kain swung through to pick up some stuff he stashed at their crib and dropped off a couple bricks of Commercial weed and a pound of Dro. He used their place from time to time as a stash spot.

It was the first-time Damien saw so many different kinds of drugs in one spot. He saw a key of powder broken down into eight bags called Big-eights; 10, hundred-packs of OXYs, 30, hundred-packs of E. Damien was in shock. He couldn't believe what his eyes were seeing. Kain was a hustler but apart from the way Kain looked and dressed, he did not act like one.

Kain surprised him, especially since before that happened Kain helped him out a few times, when it got late and Damien was too shattered to go home — Kain would let him crash at is crib and feed him. Looking out. Damien never saw him make plays. Sell drugs. After Damien saw what Kain was really about, he wanted to chill with the cat even more. Besides, Kain didn't seem to mind him being around all the time.

It was obvious to Damien that Kain treated him as he would his own son, if he had one. He didn't like Damien drinking or doing anything more than weed, and he didn't even like that. And absolutely *no* cigarettes! Kain didn't hound him, though. He simply told him, "You can't trust anyone, especially someone who does drugs, man."

Damien tolerated his rules because the cat seemed to care about him, when everyone else didn't, especially his parents. He wasn't like other hustlers Damien had met. Kain never made the Game seem glamorous. Not at all. It was simply one of the ways he made money. Damien suspected that Kain hated every minute of it, which made Damien appreciate Kain even more for looking out for him.

Damien always wanted to become a hustler, but he didn't know anyone who could put him on. And every time he chilled with Kain, he would tell Damien how the Game was no good. And how it could turn motherfuckers into monsters.

"Money corrupts, lil man," Kain warned.

Despite Kain's discouragement, Damien still asked Kain to put him on with some weed. He would even go to him to grab dimes for cats, which Kain only did as a favor for people he knew.

Damien could remember one time when he tried to show Kain he could hustle. He went to him for a couple of dimes. Kain asked who it was for, and Damien told him it was for his friend Mike, when it was for this cat named Freddie, who had beef with Kain. Damien had taken too long, so Freddie knocked on Kain's door looking for him. Freddie thought Damien had run off with his money. It was funny considering it was the kind of shit Freddie would pull.

Freddie asked for Damien, while he kept his distance by backing down the stairs as he spoke.

"Yeah, *what's up,* dawg?" Kain asked. "What 'cha want?"

"Is that kid Damien here?" Freddie asked, keeping his distance. Kain was puzzled for a moment. "Yeah, he'll be right out."

"Hey, wait!" Freddie said, as the door began to close.

Kain pulled the door back open. The expression on Kain's face said: WHAT? And to his surprise the-*what*-was not expected. Freddie wanted to squash the beef between them. Kain who would rather an ally than a foe accepted. When Kain went back into the room where Damien was bagging shit up, his young friend was visibly nervous. He heard everything that was said between Kain and Freddie, including that Freddie thought that he had run off with his money.

Damien knew they had beef. To make matters worse, he lied. However, he didn't see anything wrong with what he had done. He only lied so Kain could get the money. *What's wrong with that*?

Damien knew Kain would never have served Freddie. He just didn't see anything wrong with it, but Kain did. Damien could feel the tension in the air when Kain entered the room. After a moment, he calmly spoke:

"That was Freddie," Kain said. "You almost done? He's waiting outside…and…dawg, why did you lie?" He shook his head, reconsidering the last question. "Well, never mind, son. Just don't ever do something like that again, ya heard?" He paused for a moment. "I don't like liars, not at all, you feel me?"

Damien nodded.

"I should tell you not to come back, especially since you *knew* we had beef. But he squashed that shit and so will I." He shook his head. "Just don't do that again, alright?"

Damien of course had to react with his emotions and not his intelligence.

"I don't need this shit, but I'm sorry, dawg," he said in a huff. "But, I just don't see the issue. All I…saw…was you losing money."

"Of course you didn't, or you wouldn't have done it. And that's why I'm *telling* you, because I do, alright? Besides I don't need no thirty dollars…I got plenty believe that. Now, go serve him and come right back."

As Damien headed for the door, upset his boy just yelled at him, Kain said, "Lil man, *One*."

"One," Damien said, as he left the house knowing it was over. A smile spread across his face. He did wrong. Kain said his peace and that was that.

A few weeks after that incident, Kain to Damien's surprise, put him on big for a youngin. But *damn*, the rules were strict. However, Kain knew his shit, so Damien didn't mind. Kain taught him the ways of the Game and he learned well.

Damien even got a job at Da Urban Clothing Store up at the mall. Kain telling him: "You *need* a legit source of income. How you gonna have all this money and no job. Now that's hot!" *This cat was real*, he thought.

Damien started moving two pounds of weed a week for Kain. He never charged Damien that much. A few pennies on the dollar. Kain didn't like weed or anything small. It was just too hot for him. So he let Damien move the green. This setup went on for almost two years. Well, more like 18 months, and in that time, Kain indeed became like a father to Damien—helping him with whatever problem arose that needed serious attention.

After Kain put Damien on, he went back to the block like always, except now he was on the come up, pumping weed to anyone who was looking for it. At first, he just thought it would give him some spare change and something to blaze. But Da Brickz had other plans for him...and so did the Game.

From the start, he moved heavy for a 14-year-old off the rip. Two pounds, all in 2.5 gram dimes, when everyone else sold under 1.8. The product wasn't bad for what it was. Damien didn't care. He was on his way. Where he was going, he didn't know, nor did he care.

Damien thought Kain just did things around the way and didn't know the size of his operation. It never crossed his mind that he did anything up in the city as well. Despite the fact that he knew Kain from the city, and that Kain brought him up there to visit while Kain visited with his own people. He should have known—Kain had customers everywhere. Damien started to think that Kain moved shit out of state too. Something he gathered from a conversation Kain had on his cellphone.

On the block, as well as other parts of town, Damien put on his people. His boy Jimmy knew older cats that puffed, but those cats only copped quarters to ounces. They became Jimmy's people. At first, anyone wanting anything more than a dime had to get it from either Jimmy or Damien. Dez was too much of a pothead to be serving customers. *Monkeys can't sell bananas.* Since he knew everyone who smoked, he brought in the customers. Crazy E and Desaun became their enforcers.

They were young, so some of the older cats would try to stick them. Crazy E was fourteen but big for his age at six feet two-hundred-and-forty pounds. Desaun was eighteen and big: Six-four two-hundred-and-thirty pounds. He was known to be thorough (tough, you know he got it in), and he tucked heat. Damien's man Ty, although he lived on the block, knew cats all over, because he went to a different school. The girls got down too. Whitney, a chick from across town, and his girl Kim did their thing. They met Whitney through Kim. And home girl was thorough, no doubt about it. She became Fam. That was their crew and within three months Damien doubled his weight, which wasn't shit really, except to him. It allowed him to personally do next to nothing — separating himself from the business.

Time passed quickly and Da Brickz were taking Damien to a new level. He was almost fifteen. He had a job and a hustle. Life was good! However, with the good comes the bad. Damien started to see that things weren't right. Not at all. He had way too many people moving shit on the block. Not to mention: "You should never shit where you eat." At least that's what Kain had told him. "The problem wasn't weed, it was greed."

Damien had started moving other shit too on the block, against Kain's wishes. In return, the block got hot. D-boys were everywhere searching motherfuckers posted up on the block. Finding nothing but a Dutch or two. You had to do things on the low…and have lookouts. The D-Boys were crazy creeping through Da Brickz. They would even try asking motherfuckers where they got their shit from. *Like motherfuckers were gonna tell them shit.*

Don't get it wrong. Some people got knocked. Luckily not them. The block got hot as hell. To make matters worse, Damien's crew began to move more and more weight. Damien's man wouldn't let him touch coke, so he was stuck moving all kinds of weed: Commercial, Dro, and Haze. And he moved some E as well.

Kain didn't like the block where he laid his head to be hot, so there were consequences. Since every action has an equal and opposite reaction, Damien, was told by Kain, to cut back his plays. He could only keep five to ten customers. At one point, he had forty. Damien had to sell product to his people, that's it, and they had to move it *off* the block.

Christmas came and went along with Damien's birthday. In March tragedy struck, when Jimmy got knocked bringing two P's to an old-head. He had big man bail Jimmy out, but Jimmy was on probation and was lucky just to make bail. Jimmy had-probation for fighting some bitch-ass motherfucker in school, who went home and told his mother. A month later, after being bailed out by Kain, Jimmy went to court for the probation surrender and got a year for the violation. He, also, took a two-year deal for the two pounds that he got caught with. So no one was gonna see Jimmy on the street for about three years.

Jimmy getting locked set Damien back. Jimmy was his right-hand; his biggest customer. When he got popped, he moved like eight of Damien's fifteen pounds per week. And the only person, besides

Damien, who knew Jimmy's customers real well was Crazy E. Of course, Damien wasn't about to serve them, so he let Crazy E handle Jimmy's plays. But first, he had to make it clear to Crazy E they would always be Jimmy's people.

Damien kept his business separate from his personal life and kept it moving. He couldn't wait to see where the Game would take him and didn't have any idea what the effects on his life it was gonna have. Not that Damien ever gave it much thought.

It is easy to get in the Game, getting out was the hard part. Damien had absolutely no desire to get out. As a matter of fact, he wanted to be the largest, the illest, and most respected of them all. Damien wanted to be a drug lord. And with Kain's help, Damien felt he just might become exactly what he wanted.

Chapter Four

Summer was again approaching. Damien had been in the Game for about sixteen months. He had no choice but to change the way he was doing things. Even though Jimmy was in jail, Damien stacked some chips for him. He saved Jimmy's cut from his people. Despite that Crazy E served them while Jimmy was locked, Damien had always considered them Jimmy's, which Crazy E never liked.

Damien cuffed everyone: Crazy E, Ty, Jon-Jon, Kim, Whitney, Julio, and Dez even started doing some shit too, but not weed—just pills and shit. Damien also put his man Miguel on, up in the city of sin. Lynn. Miguel had his own team, like Damien's, with their friends up in the city doin their thing. Damien's team; the only customers that he had. He sold to no one else.

Damien's cousin eventually wanted to get some powder, coke for those that don't know. Damien talked with Kain and to his surprise Kain okayed it, but it had to go through Damien. Damien was proud of what he was doing; he was becoming the *man*.

Damien was Sixteen and going to be driving for the summer. Kain was becoming more and more like a father to him. He gave Damien one of his cars, a 90-something Honda Accord that was hooked up. Although not as much as his new Accord, which was off the chain…and he had other cars.

Kain rented a garage in town where he kept seven, no, eight nasty whips: A BMW M5, another BMW 760, a Lotus Elise, and a Porsche Carrera GT. Kain never drove these whips on the block. And NONE of the cars he stored were in his name. Kain had only three cars in his name, including the one he gave Damien.

No drugs were allowed in Damien's car because Kain explained how the D-Boys would love to catch a young cat riding dirty.

Damien had been working at the store for almost two years and that was where his family thought he earned his money. Only Kain and his team knew different. He was ballin for a 16-year-old. He had plenty of money, a nice whip, and a place to call his own. Kain had rented an apartment for Damien in the building where he lived. The apartment became where Damien kept his money and chilled.

Kain, who had to run his business, also had a couple of stash spots and safe houses in other towns. Consequently, Damien only saw Kain at work or when he came through. Kain, however, would make time for Damien if he needed him for any reason, even to chill. Besides all that, Kain was never seen *Ghost*.

Damien was out on the block chillin with Crazy E when this cat named Jamal came through, as they posted up on the stoop. Crazy E was in the middle of telling him how there were some stick up kids were making moves on cats from around the way. It was 10 PM. Crazy E and Jamal were tilted, when a car drove past and Damien's boy Rock waved to them.

"Fuck you!" Crazy E shouted at them.

"C, what's your problem, man?"

"Fuck them niggas." Crazy E said, drunkenly. "They're nothin but scrams, anyhow."

"What the hell are you talkin about, dawg?" Damien said, thinking his boy just lost it.

"Who the fuck cares 'bout some broke ass niggas, anyhow."

"Yo, man…your trippin! That was Petey and Roc, dawg," he said. "They gots their own thing goin on. Besides Roc's our boy."

Damien could tell that Crazy E could care less. *This muthafucka's trippin!*

Damien knew Crazy had been on some other shit, lately. All because he made a little change, this cat thought he was the motherfucking *man*. Damien just hoped it was the liquor talking. Unfortunately, he knew better. Crazy E may be nuts, but he was still his boy. And Crazy E was about to prove how crazy (as well as stupid) he could get.

Some cats came through from the Heights and started arguing with Jamal. Damien wasn't worried about these cats, because Fatboy, Tony T, and Ripp were harmless loud-mouth bitches who would pull rip and runs…and then get their asses beat. They wanted some money Jamal owed them for a Movado watch he got off them.

Before the argument could go any further, Crazy E, who was drinking a beer, took three crisp 100 dollar bills out of this pocket and threw the c-notes at the surprised kids, shouting "Bitches!" Then he whipped his beer bottle at them, as he pulled his ratchet, pointing it in their direction.

"Move on, muthafuckaz!" The look on Crazy E's face screamed I wished they would try something.

"Yo, *chill*, CHILL!" Tony T said, scared for the both their lives. We ain't gots no beef wit 'cha"

"Well, you do now, BITCH…. How you gonna come on *my* block! Huh, like youse some thorough muthafuckaz — when y'all straight *bitches!*"

Then with surprising speed for his size, Crazy E pistol-whiped Tony T across the face.

Damien shook his head. *Here we go.*

Jamal jumped right into action and grabbed-up Fatboy, then smashed him repeatedly with the bottom of the beer bottle until the bloodied bottle broke. At which point, Fatboy collapsed. Jamal continued stomping the shit out of him, kicking Fatboy all over. Blood was everywhere.

After Crazy E pistol-whipped Tony T, he started whaling on the kid with no mercy. Ripp, who stood there in shock, went for his heat. Damien started to go for his own. It was stashed behind a rock around the corner of one of the buildings that enclosed the stoop. Before Damien could react, Crazy E leveled his tool at Ripp and emptied it. Everyone dipped.

Someone called 911. They arrived about twenty minutes later. Surprisingly, Ripp was still alive. Barely. He was intensive care for eight days. He kept to the rules of the street—and never said a word about who shot him. He was solid. Fatboy, though, was not…so he told on Jamal for smashing the shit out of him, but said he couldn't remember who else was there, apparently afraid of Crazy E. Jamal got arrested and they questioned him for hours. Damien called Kain, who once again sent one of his attorneys to represent Jamal. The police stopped their questioning and let him go. Kain stepped in because he didn't want it coming back to the crew, especially Damien.

Kain was pissed. Crazy E, however, thought he was Superman. Kain didn't want Damien fuckin' with Crazy E anymore. However, Damien somehow convinced Kain to give him a chance to handle Crazy E himself, because he was his boy. "Look, Lil man, Kain said, with a serious expression, "If you can't handle that stupid muthafucka, I will. You hear me?"

"Yeah, dawg, I heard." Damien said, heated at Crazy E for putting him in a hot spot with Kain. "Loud and clear and I got it, alright?"

Hells no, not a spot where he wanted to be, at all.

Chapter Five

Crazy E went on the DL until things cooled down. He finally called Damien, two weeks later, saying he had Damien's money and he needed to see him. Damien told Crazy E to meet him at the mall, in case Kain decided that he needed to talk to him he could. Besides, Damien had to work.

Damien informed Crazy E that no one on the block was talking at all. Nobody seemed to know anything about that night, as if it never happened. Ripp turned out to be okay, except for his six gunshot wounds; he now wore as a badge of gangsta honor. He used them to tell war stories to other cats, pumping up his rep, but Ripp still claimed he didn't know who shot him.

Damien hoped he could handle Crazy E, because he knew Kain all too well…he'd turn the situation into a test. One thing that he had noticed about Kain was, apart from a couple of plays he had seen, you *never* saw anything he didn't *want* you to see. Which gave Damien the idea that Kain knew he wanted to hustle. And Kain just wanted to make sure, if Damien did hustle, he would do it right. He just hoped that Crazy E didn't cause a bigger problem.

Kain had eleven stores across the state in the busiest malls, with plans to open more. Damien even heard a rumor (which there were not many) that Kain was retiring from the Game and hoped he would be heir.

On the day he was to meet Crazy E, Damien arrived at the store to find that Troy, the manager of Damien's manager was given the day off. Only Kain and members of his team were in the store. Damien found out after he arrived to work, and it made him worried about Crazy E.

The thing that struck Damien as odd, was no one seemed to know that Kain was in the Game, or that he put Damien on. The streets talked; however, people didn't seem to agree whether Kain was a retired Baller or that he now made his money solely from his stores. The one thing people could agree on: Damien was family to Kain. Therefore, respected and protected.

"I already grabbed the eight pounds Crazy E needs," Kain said and then explained what he had planned — but not why his crew was at the store.

Damien had put new gear out on the floor, some new Rocawear shit, as well as some sick Fishscale shirts. Damien, of course was crisp from head to toe, since day one, thanks to Kain. He believed you always needed to be crisp.

"Yo, Baby, you need to dress for success, Lil man, remember that," Kain said, "because people will always remember how you looked to them."

Damien agreed, for he always remembered how Kain looked to him. *Crisp.*

Kain knew the Game, and he knew it well. He was never wrong when it came to matters concerning this thing of theirs. And, of course, Damien hated it. But when it came to hustling, Kain knew his shit. No one could ever say he didn't, even if he went down he'd just be another ghetto legend.

Damien glanced over the rack, to check the time. It was going on 7 PM and he had told Crazy E to be there at 6:30, because that was when he went on break. Instead, Damien finished stocking the merchandise. Crazy E finally showed up at 7:40.

Before Crazy E showed up, Kain called Damien over to talk. .

"Hey, Lil man, come here!"

"What's up dawg?"

"Come on over here," Kain said. "I wanna holla at 'cha, for a minute, it won't take long."

"Alright, dawg, but I gots lots of stuff to put away," he said, knowing how much Kain liked hard workers. He approached Kain, "What's goin on?"

"Look you're my man, right?" Kain said, asking an obvious question.

"Yeah, of course, dawg. You know it."

"Well, unless you get a handle on this cat, I'm gonna have to handle it myself. Can't have some stupid ass kid making shit hot. I just can't, feel me?"

"I know, man! I'll talk to him, I *told* you he's coming by to meet up with me, here."

"I remember, *you* got that," Kain said. "Handle your biz, just remember, though, we fam. This cat ain't shit to me. He may be your *fam*, and that's peace. But he's definitely *not* mine."

"What will happen if I can't handle this problem?"

"Maybe I'll have to cut him off. He'll get nothin and you will lose that money. Or maybe you can't handle the Game. It's a messy business. It could be you're just not ready to get down and dirty in the mud."

Damn, he's throwing it down like that!

"I thought *we* were fam?"

"We are, Lil man. You know you would be taken care of. You know that. Check it out, would you let anyone try to take me down, or out for that matter… if you knew someone was gonna try?"

"Of course, not," Damien said, angrily. "Damn, I'd do whatever was needed to stop them."

"Good. I'm happy to hear that. And you see, I won't let anything or person harm you," he paused, "and this muthafucka, I tell you, will do just that… if left unchecked."

"Alright, I'll do my best, fo real," Damien said, giving his mentor a hug. Kain was like a father to him and Damien would never let him down. "Can I get back to work?"

"Yeah, sure, Lil man," Kain said. "What you want to eat, tonight?"

"Chinese."

"Alright, I order for the food to be delivered here at 8pm, so you got some time. Oh, when's he comin to meet you?"

"He supposed to be here at 6:30."

"Alright, you got about an hour and a half until he gets here…so go get your work done."

"Yeah…I'll get it done," Damien said recognizing that Kain was playing.

Kain could always make Damien feel at ease. Like, after talking with him, he could do anything like conquer the world.

Damien checked the time, only five minutes passed since the last time he checked the clock. He just wished Crazy E would chill-the-fuck-out and fall back. He would try his best to get Crazy E to listen because he was his boy. However, Kain was family and Crazy E wasn't making Damien much money. He still moved the same eight pounds Jimmy moved before he got knocked. Damien could have anyone handle them moves, but let Crazy E tell it, he was the man. The only one on the team making money.

Crazy E walked into the store at 7:40. *So like him. He always thought everything revolved around him.*

However, to Damien's relief, he found out that Crazy E was just being real paranoid. *Maybe it will all work out.*

"What up, man?" Crazy E said, giving customers he knew in the store dap.

"Not much, dawg. What you so late for?" Damien asked in a serious tone.

"I just wanted to be careful, that's all."

"Alright, that's cool, let me tell Kain I'm goin on break."

"Yeah, it's cool," Crazy E said, his eyes darting around, obviously nervous, "go do your thing."

Damien went to tell Kain, and then they left to go spark a spliff…and for Damien to air his peace.

"Yo, dawg, what's up wit you, man…seriously? You been buggin out, son," he said, before taking a toke of the spliff, holding it in as Crazy E talked.

"Yeah, kid, I know I've done did some stupid shit, dawg. But I haven't drunk in two weeks. All I've been doing is grindin my ass off."

"Oh, yeah," Damien said, not believing a thing.

"Dawg, I'm okay, fo real, I'll do *whatever* you want a muthafucka to do, dawg." He sighed. "I just lost my fuckin' mind…and I just hope things are good. Do you think I can kick it, or should I stay low?"

Damien believed he meant what he said, but only time would tell. He decided to give his boy a second chance.

"Alright dawg, but no violence, and yeah, stay fuckin' low…and I don't have to tell you, *do* I?"

"Nah, dawg, everything's cool," Crazy E stated reluctantly. "I don't want your boy mad at my stupid ass. Fuck that!" He paused. "Even I'm not that dumb." He took the spliff back for another hit.

"Look, Kain's pissed you brought heat to my doorstep and *his*," steel in his voice. "You're my boy, but you brought drama when you know we're not about no damn drama."

Damien hoped Crazy E got the Damn message, but you never could tell.

"You right, dawg," Crazy E said. "I wasn't lookin out for the crew starting shit like that." He looked straight at Damien. "I won't fuck up like that again, alright."

"Alright, my man," Damien said, hoping Crazy E was serious.

"Man, let's go do this thing of ours, nigga." Crazy E said. "Oh yeah, I'll bring my weight up too."

What's he, psychic?

Crazy E passed back the spliff. Damien took the last hit, snuffed it out, before heading back inside.

While they walked back inside, Crazy E asked, "Where's my pick-up?"

"Back in the store, *why*?"

"No reason, Dee," Crazy E said. "Just thought it was in your car or somethin."

Damien noticed a puzzled look on Crazy E's face, a slight register of fear.

"I thought the big man didn't like dirt in his store?"

"He don't, but in this case, he felt it was for the best."

"I see."

"Yeah, dawg. You fucked up…and you're lucky you're my boy, enough said."

"You ain't kiddin," Crazy E said, in a nervous tone.

You could really tell how nervous Crazy E the moment they reentered store and saw Kain.

"Wassup, Big dawg?" Crazy E said.

Kain nodded before looking at Damien. What's up kid? You two work out the problem?"

"Yeah dawg, he agreed to do what he needs to do."

Kain nodded then looked at Crazy E.

"Good," Kain said. "But you ever put my man, right here, in fuckin' situation like that again," Kain stared straight into Crazy E's soul, "you'll never have anything, ever, to worry about, feel me, dawg?"

"Yeah…*we*…cool." Crazy E said, a bit nervous.

"Good, now that that's over, let's eat."

"What we having?" Crazy E asked.

"Chinese," Damien said..

"It's in the back," Kain said, "in the break room. Let's go chill."

Crazy E was stupid for doing that crazy shit. Damien had told him no drama unless it was brought to them. He, also, knew how protective Kain was of Damien. Crazy E had seen it firsthand. They were chillin behind Kain's crib. Kain happened to be talking to someone outside their car, just kickin it, when this older cat tried to pull a rip-and-run. The motherfucker grabbed Damien's shit, punched him in the face, and then pushed him to the ground.

Kain saw it go down and snatched up the fool, beating the motherfucker half dead. And then Kain smashed the dudes' boys as well. Kain was a force to be reckoned with. Afterwards, he made them apologize to Damien. Since they were on foot, Kain had his boy give them a ride to wherever they wanted to go. *Hospital, home, wherever, their choice.*

They entered the break room. What an understatement. The room was plush from the floor up. There was a Persian rug resting on red cherry wood floors, three flat screen TVs, a pool table, video games for Play Station and XBox, a good size kitchenette, and a bathroom. There was even a Jacuzzi in another room. And you couldn't forget the Corinthian leather living room set. The *Break room* always amazed Damien, he knew Crazy E was in awe, seeing it for the first time. The place was more like a pimp's pad than a break room. Kain had them in all his stores, minus the Jacuzzi. He said it improved the quality of the work environment. In other words, people wanted to work there. His store had extremely low employee turnover. Although you had to work hard, everyone tried to get a job a one of Kain's stores.

They ate the food, getting their grub on. They were just chillin'. Kain and his boy Jayson was there, along with Kain's girl Tanisha (the same chick that used to chill with them back in the day), as well as Kain's other boy Stu-dawg. There were two more who had already eaten and were out on the sales floor working. Damien and the others watched TV or played video games. Around 9pm Kain handed Crazy E a couple of bags of gear, including what appeared to be at least four pair of size 13 kicks. The boxes were huge.

"Your p's are in these bags," Kain said, smiling. "Twenty-three of 'em. Make your moves, young buck, and get lil man back his dough."

"I will quick. I already have sixteen of them gone," Crazy E said with pride. "I just have to move the rest."

Eight were for Jimmy's people. This cat was funny. Didn't he realize Kain knew about *everything* Damien moved. *Fuck it*, Kain seemed to think it was amusing, so Damien guessed he would too. Damien believed Crazy E did realize if he didn't come up with all the money—he was done. You have to pull your own weight in this here Game, and by Kain giving Crazy E the bags himself, it *now* involved Kain. It was now out of Damien's hands.

After Crazy E left, they finished restocking the remaining displays. Damien picked out some new gear to rock. When he went to pay for it, Kain told him, "Not this time, it's on me." Kain did that more often than not, but this time he seemed like a proud father who's pleased when his kid does good.

Damien didn't know what caused it this time, but maybe it was because he had done all his work, placed his ever-increasing order, and got Crazy E to, at least, agree to slow his role. Crazy E told Kain that he would do what was needed of him to do. No Crazy shit. Kain left the store with his people, while Damien stayed behind to finish straightening out the shelves. When he was done, he locked up and went home, stopping at his crib first.

Damien's father seemed to dislike Kain for all wrong reasons. He knew Kain looked out for his son more than a typical boss would. Since his father was a bartender, he knew two things: Damien was protected by Kain who was a respected drug dealer. Bartenders, especially good ones, always knew who the local dealers were. Even ones purported to be retired. Kain looked out for Damien far more than his father could, so he believed the dislike was borne out of something else. But even if his father was jealous or something else altogether, he never said a negative thing about Kain.

If he didn't know any better, he would swear his father was afraid of Kain or something. After his father found out that Damien was tight with Kain, he never got hit again. *So maybe he should be.*

When Damien got home, he stopped off at his stash pad first, his father was home, as well as drunk. Thankfully, he stayed in his room. Damien had ordered cable and a house phone, after working at the store for a while-a long time before Kain had got the apartment for him in his building.

Damien ate some of the Chinese food he brought home from work. He sat back, watched TV and talked to Kim on the phone for a little while. It was about 11:30, and he had school in the morning, so he was glad he drove 'cause he would've never made the bus. Plus, his friends needed a ride as well. He wasn't supposed to be driving anyone around. And it wasn't the police he worried about, *fuck them,* if Kain ever found out he would take away his ride.

"I won't give you a burner," Kain said, "but you want a bigger weapon…25-hundred pounds of one?"

Damien had said, "Hell, yeah!"

The result was Kain made Damien do all these driving courses and drove with him. Damien did it all and was glad he did. Driving was fun, but it was also a responsibility.

As he watched reruns of UFC, he fell asleep. He was glad that, even with the Crazy E situation, the day ended as good as it had.

Chapter Six

School was breaking for the summer, which would be his fifth. Damien couldn't wait. They only seemed to get better. He learned from science that every action has an equal and opposite reaction. He hoped the reaction from Crazy E's actions would somehow have a positive outcome.

Three weeks passed at the speed of light.

Crazy E made good on his word. He upped his weight to 30 pounds and started movin pills too. Things were looking good.

Kim and Damien hooked-up and things were good. Damien was happy. His crew was chill. He just worried about Crazy E and hoped he could remain laidback. Damien wasn't on the block as much. Instead he chilled at his crib.

Summer was upon them.

He officially had his license and was cruising down the highway headed for Uno's. Damien and Kim had plans to get lunch and then head to the beach.

Damien was either with Kim or work more than he was on the block. He spent less and less time on the block as time moved on. Kain kept his crib in the building, although, it became one of Damien's stash spots. Kain still had stuff in the apartment; even though, he bought a place on the beach. A private estate with an electric gate and all. Kain said he installed it 'cause he'd always wanted a big gated house like those movie gangsters." Kain's new place was luxurious. He was on top of the world.

$

A couple months had passed, and it was now the middle of summer. Kain opened six more stores in four states, and they were doing as well if not better than the ones he already had. Kain's plan now was to open at least two stores in each state per month for about a year and then expand from there. Of course, this had Damien worried because by next year he was sure Kain would be totally out the Game.

Damien was doing very well. After he realized that Kain might retire for real, he started stacking his paper; even though, he knew it wasn't necessary. Damien liked to have his own change. Money earned not given. He worked hard for his money, whether it was at the store or in the Game.

Kain told Damien that when he turned eighteen, which was in a year and a half, he would be promoted to manager, if he kept up what he was doing. Damien practically ran the store already. Kain was expanding and he would be promoting Troy to District manager. Kain had plans and was preparing Damien to step up.

Damien wondered who would take over his other business. He figured a cat like that couldn't just retire and leave people hungry. He was sure Kain had a plan. Damien hoped Kain would hand it down to him; however, he knew Kain had people who have been in the Game for many years.

The summer didn't seem as live as the past ones had been, probably because he wasn't hanging out on the block as much. Damien was almost seventeen, but felt much older.

When Damien got to Uno's and seated in a booth by the window. Kim told him about the new car her mom just got, as a birthday gift, from Kim's stepfather. *Damien couldn't wait until he could do that kind of thing for Kim.*

Kim was beautiful and getting more so by the moment, but what interested him more was her intelligence. Damien wondered from time to time if she would be with him if he was broke. Kim knew what he did. Shit, she did it too. Kim and her girls were movin a good amount of weight, so his thoughts were fleeting. She was with him for him.

"Baby…whats ya wanna do wit 'cha life?" Damien paused to look out the window. "We can't run them Brickz forever."

"Go to college, open up a business…I don't know, grow old wit you!"

With that infectious smile of hers, she winked at Damien. He knew she was special. They finished their lunch and went about their day.

They had fun at the beach. He headed to work after dropping Kim off at her house. It was Friday, and the new school-year fast approached, the mall was packed and the store had crazy business. It seemed as though everyone bought their gear at Da Urban Clothing Store. There was hardly room to move around.

Kain was there, an unusual sight, since he was either opening new stores or searching for new brands to put in them. He even came out with his own, exclusive, line of gear, which was very expensive, which didn't bother anyone, seeing people wanted it. Bad. The gear was hot. It being exclusive to Kain's stores made it more desirable, but you had to be a baller to afford it. The most expensive hip hop clothes Damien had ever seen.

When Damien got to the store, Troy told him where he was most needed. The night was crazy with people coming through the store. Before Damien knew it, the clock read 10:30…and he was beat.

On his way home, he stopped by the stoop to check on his team. Everything was good, so he parked his whip and went up to the crib. On the way up, he stashed some cash at Kain's place. Damien still thought of it as the big guys.

In his apartment, Damien threw his keys on the kitchen counter before going into the living room to watch TV. After he got comfortable, he ordered a pepperoni pizza. When it arrived, Damien wasted no time demolishing the entire thing. Dez stopped by to drop off some cash. They smoked a blunt. After, Damien dipped across the street to his father's.

His father was home and *not* in his room. They watched TV for a while and talked—something they didn't do too often. During the conversation Damien's father told him that he was doing good and to keep up the good work. It was the closest, up to this point, his father had ever come to say he was proud. His father didn't say too much, but it was enough. After his father went off to bed, Damien continued to watch television.

His cell phone sang, "Sweet love of mine!" Damien answered the call knowing that it was Kim.

"What's up, baby? Damien said, sounding a bit exhausted.

"Nothin…just want to talk to my Boo," she said in her best sexy voice. They talked about everything, and nothing, for about an hour. She also told him that she and her girls were out.

The Game had them good. He had just given her ten pounds. *She was out but how?* He knew her Pops had something to do with it, but damn his girl could move her weight.

It turned out that Kim's father had a friend who hit a drought. Her father told his long-time friend that he may be able to help him out. They charged him up some but the price was still cheaper and better in quality than what he usually got. The guy wanted twenty more and at least twenty every week.

Kim asked if they could handle that much product. They could and would. *Damien did wonder what happened to this guy's connect.* The answer came in the morning's newspaper: Two hundred pounds of marijuana was confiscated in a DEA raid of an auto dealership; they had a shipment coming in, and it was discovered by Border Patrol crossing over from Canada. The driver agreed to assist the authorities with the delivery of the marijuana. They all got knocked. Caught red-handed.

Damien didn't know the cats, but he knew it helped his business.

Chapter Seven

Christmas came fast. The months melted away as the ground began to freeze. *Damn, time flew by*. He'd be seventeen in a few days and he could hardly wait. Although he and his dad made amends, Damien decided to move over to the other crib. It actually strengthened their bond. They did more things together after he moved out then when he lived with his pops. Kain transferred the apartment into Damien's name. He was there most of the time anyway. He seldom went home. Kim and Damien would stay over there.

Damien had a great Christmas with his dad, mom, and two brothers. The next day he spent time with Kain and his wife Tanisha, along with his extended family to celebrate the holiday. Kain always celebrated Christmas the day after. Kim and Damien even had a gathering at their crib for the team. *Life was good*.

Once Damien turned seventeen, time wouldn't let him catch his breath. Time just kept moving faster. Before he knew it, he had two more birthdays, and he was nineteen and his man Jimmy was coming home. Damien could hardly wait for his boy to hit the brickz. Jimmy heard Damien was doin *BIG THANGS*. He even wrote Damien asking if Kain retired because he heard rumors that he had. It wasn't true but it was for the best people believed he had. He started to doubt that Kain would retire though he mentioned the possibility several times.

Jimmy was grateful Damien kept it real by writing and keeping his canteen stacked while he did his time in county. Jimmy had run into people who thought Damien was doin "BIG THANGS," despite not having any idea what he was doing. These cats claimed to somehow be down. Like Jimmy wouldn't check. *Dumb-asses*.

Damien waited to tell Jimmy that he had stacked his cut since he got locked. He had at least 70k for him to come home to. Not bad for a bunch of youngins.

Damien was stackin his crazy paper. He put about 70 percent of his paycheck in the bank and lived on some of the street money. Kain gave Damien bonuses, which also went right into his savings. His paycheck and bonuses eventually went straight into his account: Direct deposit. And he started investing in the stock market.

He had to be the only nineteen-year-old in Da Brickz with over a 100K in the bank legally. His credit was off the hook. He had a real platinum card and an American Express Green and Blue card. Not to mention twenty safe deposit boxes and ten safes elsewhere, with more than 450k that he never touched. Ever. *Not bad for a bunch of youngins.*

Damien, after reading the book *Blow*, worked with 150K he kept in a hidden safe at the crib. He wanted for nothing.

Damien was movin over 200 pounds of weed a week. You didn't have to do the math to know that it was a lot. He didn't know exactly how much he had, though he believed that he could never spend it all. His youthful naivety worked in his favor. Besides if you added the five birds a week, along with the eight to nine thousand pills of assorted kinds he now moved. He *was* doin it BIG.

The Game was fun and he lived for the thrill of it. However, it could be very demanding. He thought about getting out, and even mentioned it to Kain. He was making him some serious paper now, so he didn't think Kain would want him to get out of the Game. Despite the money, Kain thought he should and gave him several reasons: He had plenty stashed away; A good job with a promising future in Kain's company, which expanded faster than originally expected. East of the Mississippi he had stores in every state. He also had stores in Texas and California. Kain was thriving. Damien didn't need to hustle. Neither did Kain.

They were alike in many ways. It was as if Damien was the updated digital version of the analog Kain.

Crazy E still laid down his gangsta wherever he went. He also insisted that he wasn't giving up any of *his* customers: "They mines now!"

Crazy E didn't hang with them anymore. He had got his own people over the years. He was just being

Crazy E. Damien told him if that's what he wanted then it wouldn't be a problem. "You sure dawg; that's what you want?" Crazy E told him there was no other way about it. Damien was relieved that was all Crazy E wanted.

He still needed to talk to Jimmy, before he decided where to put him, although he knew where he needed him most. Three years locked up could turn mother-fuckers away from the Game. But since Crazy E would be getting what he wanted, he didn't want to hear any shit from him. It was his business and no one could tell him what to do, except maybe for Kain who without him Damien would have nothing.

Crazy E was a loose cannon. However, he kept his warring ways off the block, at least most of the time. It was only a matter of time before he lost it completely. One of Damien's original members had left to go do his own thing through another connect. Damien was heated at first, but friends are better than enemies, so he let it go. Crazy E, on the other hand, wanted to nod the motherfucker just for leaving the team. Crazy E always reacted in the most extreme way possible. Damien didn't see the logic in this way of thinking.

After the controversy with Rip had died down, Crazy E went right back to being himself. Gangsta. He acted as though he was unstoppable. Damien tried to talk to him, but Crazy E only told him what he wanted to hear. The problem was that crazy E thought he did more for Damien than he actually did.

When Crazy E came to talk to Damien about Jimmy getting out and his plays, he believed his own hype: "Who holds you down, dawg?" he said. "I do! No one else move that weight. No one but me."

Crazy E had no fuckin' clue about how much the team moved or who moved what. He thought because the only name you heard on the street was his own meant that the rest of the team moved shit. He would shit if he knew that Kim and Whitney's team moved five times more product than he did and with absolutely no drama. Anyone who questioned or disagreed with Crazy E would get their head smashed-in, right in the middle of the street. He even started shooting up the block in the broad daylight. Straight disrespecting Kain.

Damien knew Crazy E was playing with fire, so he tried to warn him. "Kain's gonna flip, so you need to slow your roll."

"Fuck Kain! He ain't in the Game no more. He went soft dawg…it's us now!"

Crazy E was so damn stupid. Kain was Kain. You only saw what he wanted you to see.

Chapter Eight

Kain walked into his new office, hung up his coat, and sat behind his desk. His personal assistant followed behind with some papers that needed his signature. The ten-year lease renewals were for the stores he had in 200 malls across the North East. The Urban Clothing Store chain was growing exponentially by the minute. Kain's intricate plan to wash his money through his stores worked flawlessly.

He was a success a story to be packaged and sold to the public: "Ex-con becomes Clothing Store Chain Mogul." King magazine even did a piece on him. It had taken nine years to pull it all together. The hardest part was maintaining control of the business while he was in Norfolk State Prison, but he made it through it all.

Now that things were in place it was time for Kain to close his other venture. None of his original people needed to hustle anymore. The original ten either worked for him or had their own businesses. No, he was sure his people wanted to retire from the Game as well. Not many got the chance, and Kain figured he better do it while he still could.

He was realistic and believed that the young cats under his protégé or the ones under his people would see things differently. Closing down shop was no option for him anyhow. How do you stop 4,000 brickz during a slow week? Never mind that, he also moved two and a half tons of weed and another ton of pills. *No, you couldn't unless you wanted to be dead.*

There would have to be an executive reconstruction: teams would need new leaders and someone would have to take his place.

It was hard to believe that Kain only had ten customers, besides Damien, who made eleven. His product was everywhere, coast to coast. It would be nice if his people could just work directly with his South American connect. However, Kain knew that he would probably have to pass the reigns on to someone else. *But who?*

Kain had conflicting feelings, for he wanted Damien to takeover, but he also wanted him to retire as well. The Game was no place for a brilliant youmg mind such as Damien's. No, he knew Damien could do far more than just run them streets caught up in the Game. Kain wanted him to help run his vast enterprise that now occupied the building that he was in, where his corporate office was now located. Damien didn't need to be on those unforgiving streets anymore. *Yeah right, Dee give up them brickz. Now he was dreaming.*

Damien was young. He liked Da Brickz. In time, Kain only hoped he would change, before it was too late. A while back, Damien did ask Kain what he thought about him getting out, but that frame of mind didn't last long. Kain had seen too many souls get lost to the Brickz. He didn't want that for Damien. Kain had been caught up with his company's expansion, so he had only seen Damien but twice in the past month. *He'll have to fix that.*

Everything had him going crazy—the price of success. He ran a private company that took in over 90-million dollars. It had its challenges and things didn't go as he expected but it worked. Kain was set for life. He had arrived providing that the Game didn't fuck things up on him, the way it had a habit of doing.

Chapter Nine

Damien was eating at a restaurant on the waterfront called the Spot. It was where you could find him at lunch time and after work. To the patrons, the place was managed by a friend of Damien and Kain's. In reality, it was owned by them. It was Damien's baby. No one knew that they owned any part of the restaurant. People just thought, what they wanted them to think, that they were just a friend of the restaurateur, Jon.

The restaurant turned into a hot nightclub when the sun went down. They had either a premier DJ or a live act. It was the place where Damien could unwind and just relax. He had gotten tired of staying in the crib all the time. He no longer liked to post up on the block, for too long. The Spot became his chill spot.

He glanced around at all the people in the Spot. Jimmy's coming-home bash. A private party for his man. No one could get into the Spot without one being invited and two having a special ticket that was made specifically for them. Jimmy was having a good time.

Jimmy was grateful for all that Damien had done for him while he was away. Damien grew cheerful at the next thought. Jimmy had no idea he had stacked

70 grand for him, and got him a crib. Damien hoped his boy would take over for a while, so Damien could enjoy life—and take Kim on a much-needed vacation.

Having Jimmy back home felt like he never left. He had gained weight and gotten very muscular while inside. Jimmy wasn't much taller than Damien, but now he was ripped.

The turnout for Jimmy's coming-home-bash was huge. They had three hundred names on the guest list. Once everyone on the list arrived, just for fun, they told the bouncers to let in straight dimes, no dudes. Besides the females, no one else was admitted. Letting the girls in wasn't the best idea but it was entertaining. After about fifteen girls, Damien stopped it. His team was there under one roof. Not a good idea to let anyone in that wasn't vetted first. Damien's team had worked on the DL since the beginning, but since these new cats called the Outside Boys came to town there has been nothing but drama. And of course Crazy E found himself at center of it all.

Jimmy danced with a chick Damien had never seen before. She was gangsta chic: Meaning she rocked haute couture, like Versace with Urban clothing, like Rocawear, mixing both styles. She looked real good and could dance.

After Jimmy got done dancing with the fine-ass sister and getting her number, he came over to Damien's booth. Damien was sitting by himself. Kim and Whitney had passed Jimmy on the way to the dance floor. Crazy E was at the bar with some cats Damien didn't know.

His team, which everyone in the brickz started calling "Da W8 Movaz," [The Weight Movers] had sub teams. Crazy E had the Crazy 8s; Kim and Whitney had the Dime Pack, for obvious reasons; Julio and Dez had their own nameless team, but they had their own business. This thing of theirs was getting bigger by the moment. 2012 was already lit.

Damien had bought a new ride. Since on paper he could afford it, he copped Kain's old '01 M5. However, he had Dez and Julio hook up his '97 Honda Accord at their shop, Coastal Customs. Everyone around the way got their cars hooked up by them. They were real good, and that's what he drove to the club that night.

Jimmy dropped heavily into the booth and rested his head on his crossed arms. He raised his head grinning. "Damn this here party is off the mutha-fuckin hook, for real kid!" He shook his head. "Thanks for holdin me down while I was away.

"No problem," Damien said, taking a sip of his drink before adding, "It's nothing…I 'm 'pose to do that, dawg."

"Yeah, I know, but come on Dee, how many really do? There are a lot of cats who were doin the damn thing in there, and who are broke as shit." Jimmy said, happy he wasn't one of them.

"'cause their peeps didn't keep it real. Who was that you were dancing wit?" Nodding to the dance floor. "See you haven't lost your game," he said laughing while he gave Jimmy dap.

"Oh, you saw that, dawg. That was Veronica, damn she's bad, right?"

"Yeah, no doubt, man, she bad."

"One more thing, good looks for that fat knot you gave me when you picked my ass up."

"Well, my brother, if you thought that was something," Damien said pausing dramatically, "what would you say if I told you I stacked your cut the whole time?"

"Yeah, right! You serious?" Jimmy said, shaking his head. "Get outta here."

"Yup…big bro," Damien said smiling, "I got like seventy stacks for you."

"See what I mean, nigga! That's the shit I'm talkin about. You real my muthafuckin dawg. Damn, no one does that shit. Nobody. You keep it real, though."

"Look, I like to think everyone on our team would do the same."

"Now…you are dreamin, but who knows."

"Well, that's not all either, but you'll have to wait until tomorrow."

"Another surprise, dawg? Aight, that's cool."

"So what are you gonna do now you out?"

"Get to husltlin, I guess. Why, what's up?"

"I want you to chill wit me, so you can see how I do everything. Also I got you a job at the store. I'm the manager now, in case you didn't know."

"Damn, kid, you do it all…huh?"

"Yeah, you know it; you have to, feel me."

"Yeah, I feel you. What 'cha got in mind?"

"Well, I can't tell you all of it yet, but if you can handle all the dumb shit, I got a job for you."

"Aight, sounds good, kid. I got you."

"Good, because I promised Kim we would take a vacation. She wants to go to Aruba and maybe tour the Caribbean, so I need someone to watch the shop."

"Like I said, I got you, but why not someone else."

"Because you're calm, and Crazy E doesn't do business the way I like."

"What 'bout everyone else?

"They got their own shit to handle, so I think you're my best bet, at least for my vacation." Damien flashed an impish smirk, as Jimmy just stared at him, lost for words.

Jimmy believed it was just a temporary gig, so Damien could take on a vacation, but to Damien it was more like a trial run. If Jimmy could handle the job, it would allow Damien to do all the things he wanted to do. He really felt that with Jimmy's help that he could. Damien had talked with Kain about his plan and he agreed.

After Kim came back to the booth from dancing, Jimmy took off to mingle with his guests while Damien chilled with Kim. About an hour later, Damien checked the time and saw that it was getting late. He talked to Kain every day on the phone, a habit since he first started chilling with the big guy. *Where's Kain?*

Kain always did what he said he was going to do, and it was almost 12:30 AM when he showed up. Damien could see the big man moving through the crowd toward the booth.

"What's good?" Damien said, as Kain approached. "Why you so late, everything aight?"

"Yeah couldn't be any better," Kain said smiling ear-to-ear. "You got a little brother."

"You serious? Tanisha had a boy?"

"Yeah, dawg, I think it was her...hmm? Yup it was."

Damien knew that he was only with Tanisha and nobody else. He was happy for him. Damien had been so busy that he had forgotten that Tanisha was pregnant. He was also happy that everything was all right. Kain couldn't stay long because he had to swing by the hospital early in the morning.

"So dawg what's his name? Damien asked

Everyone at the table waited for the answer.

"Keith."

"Aight...that's a good name, dawg," Damien said picking up his of champagne the waitress just brought everyone.

"A toast, to my lil brother and his proud father."

Everyone raised their glasses to toast.

"Saluté," Kain agreed, and they touched glasses.

"I'm the happiest man alive, right now, except for maybe Jimmy, life could get no better."

Everyone laughed and smiled. Jimmy hugged the big guy.

"You ain't kiddin, big man," Damien said, realizing he had never seen Kain so happy, as he was right now.

Everyone in the Spot congratulated him, and Kain being Kain did what he did best: He showed his gratitude by buying everyone in the place a drink and toasted to a new life. It was late. Kain had to go, they all said their goodbyes and he left to go home

Kim and Damien also decided to go home. The night had been a good one. They partied their ass's off. It was a perfect coming-home bash, as there ever was. Jimmy got to see everyone he knew, from his family to the team. Damien was also able to talk to him about his plans. He told Jimmy he'd pick him up in the morning around nine.

Damien was happy to have his boy back home. Jimmy was his right-hand, and as far as he was concerned would always be. Damien could hardly wait to see his boy's face when he sees Damien's other surprise.

Chapter Ten

Damien could hardly wait to pick up Jimmy at his mother's and bring him over to his other surprise he had in store for him. He had gotten Jimmy an apartment down the street from his own. Damien even put it under a false name, which was easily done, since Kain had been buying property like it was just another pair of kicks. He had apartment buildings all over town and several scattered about the state. His smartest move was buying all those brownstones in Boston's South End. The Buildings were rented by a property management company controlled by his family. The building that Damien lived in was owned by Kain.

He had been suspicious about his building but only found out after Kain told him about his holdings. Kain was a smart man with a solid business plan.

Jimmy was ready, with a killer hangover, when Damien picked him up in the M5. Jimmy couldn't believe that Damien owned one, even a used one that was a decade old. They pulled into the driveway of a building on Damien's street that housed Jimmy's new crib.

They got out and went into the building, when they got to the second floor, Damien unlocked the door and entered the ghetto-plush apartment: Flat-screen TVs, shiny new appliances, and plush leather furniture. The place was furnished by Damien, pimped out, yet tasteful.

"Who's crib is this, dawg?" Jimmy asked suspiciously, as he sat down heavily on the plush leather couch.

"Yours," he said smiling at his best friend.

"Not what I was thinking, but come on, dawg. You can't be serious." Jimmy said.

Damien was more than serious.

"I told you that I had another surprise for you: SURPRISE!"

Jimmy ran through the place checking it out. He then came back into the living room where Damien sat.

"Hey, Brother, one more thing." Damien handed Jimmy a shoebox. He took the box, placed it on the glass coffee table that separated them. He opened it, his mouth opened, inside were stacks of Benjamins.

"There's a hundred thou in there, live a little." Jimmy's cut had been only 70 thousand, but Damien rounded up. Happy to have his right-hand man back.

"Dawg, you just full of surprises."

They left the crib to go take care of some things, and to take Jimmy shopping for some gear and whatever else he needed. During their time together,

Damien explained how his business now worked — he even made a few moves with Jimmy. The rest of the day was uneventful, until they got to work.

They arrived just after 1 PM Christy had opened the place at 10 AM. She was a pretty young woman the same age as Damien. She lived in a neighboring town. She wasn't stuck up but she wasn't hood either. A good employee to be sure. Damien introduced Christy to Jimmy the minute they arrived and got right to work. The store was already packed. Damien had just gotten used to the store's major success. Jimmy, though, is in awe. He thought Kain must be caking it up now. No doubt about it.

Kain made sure that all the stores had the hottest items. No other urban store could compete. Damien assumed that all the traffic in and out of the store was the result of one of their new radio and TV ads. The TV spots were top quality like the big chains, and not those TV versions that were substandard, these were shot on film and not video.

It turned out to be a long day. Christy ended up staying until closing. They stopped working at 9 PM to eat dinner. Damien ordered pizza, as well as some munchies. Jimmy liked the break room and something else as well — Christy. The feeling seemed to be mutual. Damien liked the idea; the two good people who would appreciate each other. They clicked from the start and she even offered him a ride home.

It had been a long day, so Damien told his boy to go ahead and take the ride. Damien had a lot of things to do before he could leave and he saw no reason to keep Jimmy with him.

When Damien finally hit the block around 11:30 PM, he saw some of his people, so he pulled over to holla at them. The block was on fire. Blazing. They told Damien that Crazy E just let loose on the block about an hour or so before he got there. Five was everywhere, hurting business. His business. *Crazy E was always clappin at someone.*

He left the block and pulled into the parking lot a few buildings from the corner. As Damien walked into his building, his cell phone rang, cutting through the fading sounds of sirens and the smell of burnt gunpowder. It was Crazy E. He was drunk and defending his actions by saying some Outsiders bucked at him first. Damien could understand fully and believed that those Outside Boyz were crazier than Crazy E. And he appreciated that Crazy E called him but he should have called sooner.

A few hours later while Damien watched a movie his cell phone went crazy, buzzing itself across the coffee table. He snatched it up so it wouldn't wake up Kim, who had fallen asleep cuddled up close to him. He checked to see who it was before answering the call.

"What's up, dawg?" Damien whispered into the phone, as he gently moved Kim off him and covered her up with a throw, before going into the spare bedroom. "Alright…what's going on? Everything good?"

He hoped there were no problems.

"Nothin, *kid…it's twooo innn tha morninggg!*" Jimmy said in a sing-song voice. *"And I'm bored as hell, dawg."* The last part sounding little like Little Jon. "For real tho, dawg, you told me to call you later, so I am."

"Oh, yeah…I forgot. I thought you were callin for some other reason, thankfully it wasn't that. But why I wanted you to call though, I can't remember right now. I was gonna have you do something, but it can wait until tomorrow."

"Alright, I'll see you tomorrow."

"Walk over in the morning and you can use the Accord."

"Sounds good, kid. Thanks, dawg."

Damien hung up the phone and went back into the living room. Kim was no longer asleep on the couch, so Damien went into their bedroom--she was in the middle of an intense phone call.

"Everything cool, baby?" Damien asked.

She gave him the wait-a-minute finger sign. Not a good sign. Damien went back in the living room to shut off the lights and TV, then he decided to go into the kitchen to get something to drink. He got his drink and went back to the bedroom.

Kim was getting off the phone when Damien entered back into the room. She had a serious look on her face. He knew something was wrong.

"What's goin on baby? Everything good?"

"That was Whitney. We gots us a serious problem, baby," she said, shakily, with a worried expression on her face.

"What is it?"

"Whitney just told me that older cat Skip just tried to rape her lil sister."

"Damn Baby, she alright?" he said, before losing it. "I will kill that muthafucka!"

"You won't have to baby. She just did. That's the problem." Her eyes watered and facial features hardened.

Damien fished his cell phone out of his pocket to call the only person who could help: Kain.

Kain picked up on the third ring. "Yo, dawg," Damien said. "I need to clean up a mess. Can you help?"

"Is it serious?" Kain asked, knowing exactly what Damien meant.

"Yeah."

"Be ready. I'll be by to get you."

About five minutes later, Damien waited out front, as Kain pulled over to the curb in a car that Damien had never seen before. He jumped in the whip.

"Where do we need to go—and tell me what happened?" Kain asked in measured tone.

Damien filled him in, telling him about Skip and Whitney's little sister Tracy and then told him where to go. Kain then called two of his most trusted people. They would meet at Tracy's.

Chapter Eleven

When Damien, Kain and Kain's two man cleanup crew got inside the house, they found Whitney in a stoic condition. Tracy was shaken and afraid for her older sister. Kain took charge the moment they entered the house. He told both Whitney and Tracy to go clean and change their clothes and to put the blood-soaked ones in a large plastic bag he handed them. The girls went off to do what they were told.

Kain's boys brought all kinds of gear in duffel bags, including the plastic bags Kain gave the girls. It took Damien a minute to realize that these two professionally precise people were Kain's clean-up crew. They put Skip's corpse into a body bag and placed the knife in another. There were no houses in sight, so no one would see Kain and Damien lug out the body bag and place it in the cleaners' van, while they cleaned up the mess. The girls gave them their clothes, everything that they were wearing, including undergarments.

Damien and Kain left in the van, taking the body and bloody clothes to Kain's private aviation hangar at the local airport. Once they got there, they removed the body and put it into the back of a Robinson R44 helicopter. After the body was secured, Kain and Damien pulled the helicopter out of the hangar and prepared it for takeoff.

The cleaners showed up at 4:30 AM in the car Kain drove to Tracy's house. Kain and Damien waited until the cleaners were in the air before they left. Kain explained that the cleaners would drop the body into international waters. The body was weighted down with four 100-pound barbell plates, which just happened to be in the hangar, before the copter was pulled out.

The cleaners flew the chopper into international waters. Once they arrived, one of them unzipped the bag a little so blood would spill out to attract whatever carnivorous predators were lurking below. The pilot tipped the Robinson ever so slightly to one side, allowing his partner to roll out the heavy bag. They watched it fall into the deep darkness of the ocean below.

The cleaners called to confirm that the deed had been done, as Kain pulled pass the gate and up to his house. Damien knew he owed Kain big and understood that Kain purposely included him in the task. They were accessories to murder, which meant each one of them had a reason to keep it to themselves. Kain and Damien had a drink and Damien took the car they drove to Kain's garage near the block.

The next day Damien found out what happened. Tracy had met Skip at the beach and went back to her house to smoke a Dutch, drink, and chill. However, Skip had other plans. Around midnight, Tracy felt tired and wanted to go to bed, so she asked him to leave. Skip attacked her.

Whitney didn't feel like driving all the way home after having a couple of drinks with friends on White Horse Beach, so she decided instead to go to Tracy's for the night. When she arrived, she discovered skip attacking her little sister. She snapped and grabbed a knife from the kitchen before stabbing Skip too many times to count in the back, chest, head, and arms. No one fucks with fam.

Damien had Kim go over to Whitney's crib in the morning to check on her. Whit was handling it like the gangsta chick she was. She had been drunk the night before, so she was still trying to sort out what happened. Damien wasn't worried too much about her, but he *was* worried about Tracy.

After he spoke with Tracy, however, his concerns were erased. He and Kim went over to check on her as well. Damien drove his own car, so he could make some moves on the way over. Kim had asked him to out a hold on the Dime Packs order until she could talk to Whitney.

Damien got to Tracy's several minutes after Kim. He had stopped at a gas station with a Dunkin Donuts. He got gas and then went inside to D&D's, using his cellphone at the counter to take Kim and Tracy's orders.

After he arrived, he talked to Tracy.

The only thing that upset her was that someone had tried to attack her and she was helpless to defend herself. Damien suggested she take up martial-arts or boxing. Tracy said she was going to join a martial-arts school. Damien told her about one he knew in town, Dosin Kwan Martial-Arts, that he knew was good. The instructor was a friend of Kain's.

As far as what her sister did for her, she believed the motherfucker got what he had coming. Plain and simple. No matter if you came from the city or a town, only those who come from the streets, or understood getback. An eye for an eye. It may not always be the best option but in this case homeboy would have lost his life regardless. *Nobody messes with fam.*

Chapter Twelve

Damien no longer took drastic measures that were unnecessary. He hoped that Skip problem was as dead as his corpse, but sometimes things had unintended consequences. He hoped this was not one of those times. After he was as satisfied things were good, he left Tracy's to go over to Kain's mansion to see Tanisha and the baby, who were coming home from the hospital. He couldn't wait to see his lil brother for the first time.

People that aren't street, or from Da Brickz, would say that "Kain ain't your father and his son ain't your brother." Damien found this funny because the same people would claim to be fam. He learned young which emotion was behind those kinds of statements—jealousy. He didn't care what people thought; they were family to him and that was all that mattered.

As Damien approached Kain's house, he used a remote to open the gate. The huge gate slid to the right, allowing him through, it shut automatically as his car barely passed the threshold. He made his way up the drive, parking in his space next to a titanium Lamborghini, Kain's new Mercielargo.

Damien entered the house. A house keeper told him that his family was out back in the screened enclosed section of the terrace.

Tanisha and her newborn were enjoying the breeze coming up the embankment from the ocean. His baby brother was small, five pounds or so. It was one of the reasons Damien had forgotten Tanisha was pregnant. The baby had the most beautiful bluish-green eyes Damien had ever seen. Kain was a proud poppa, smiling ear to ear. He was happy for Tanisha and Kain.

Tanisha was more than a dime piece; she put most women out with her beauty and smooth ways. She was caring but also never took shit from anyone. Kain and Tanisha were cuddling on a seated swing, rocking back and forth. The baby wide-eyed silently looking around.

Tanisha told him he could pick up the baby, but Damien passed because the baby looked so delicate. Tanisha got off the swing, picked up the newborn, having none of that. She cradled him in her arms, making faces at the lil homie, "Keith," she said, as she handed him to Damien, "Here, meet, *your* big brother."

Damien carefully held the newborn, as he made a fool out of himself; the way people do when a baby is in their presence, making silly cooing sounds. He wasn't sure if he wanted to bring such a beautiful being into such an imperfect world. After he held Keith for a few minutes, he gave his baby brother back to Tanisha, and the three of them talked for a while about nothing in general except maybe for life. *He wondered whether he and Kim would ever have children.*

Kain and Damien then took a walk down to the beach. During their stroll Kain confided in Damien, for the first time, that he might retire from the Game.

"It won't be immediately, things like this take time, at least a few years. When I know for sure, I will let you know. The teams will stay in place, at least that is my hope. Damien, I know you love this business but I believe you should do the same."

Damien remained silent, because he knew that Kain was right, it was time for the big man to retire before the Game retired him. But as for himself, he wasn't sure the game would let him go so easily.

After the big talk, Damien explained to him the role he wanted Jimmy to take. Kain agreed that having Jimmy oversee Da W8 Movaz was a great idea. He also told Kain that he wanted to take Kim on a months-long vacation to the Caribbean. Kain also agreed that he should get away for some time and asked who would manage the store while he was gone. He told him that Christy could do it and that Jimmy would be there to help. Kain saw no problem with Damien's well thought out plan and told him he should go ahead with his travel plans.

Chapter Thirteen

Damien stared out across the bay, thinking about what he should do. He wanted to go on vacation. He had never wandered too far from home. His only experience outside the state was the time he had gone to Disney World and Universal Studios a few years back with Kain and a couple of his friends.

Nothing should happen that Jimmy couldn't handle. Jimmy was quickly learning everything he needed to know. Damien was sure he could handle any situation that arose while he was gone.

Tracy recovered quickly and joined Dosin Kwan Martial-Arts. She seemed happy. *Good for her.*

Whitney also was back to her old self. She would have to deal with taking a life, which was not an easy thing to erase from your conscience. However, she knew that she could never change what she did, so she moved on with life. The Dime Pack's numbers were even more impressive than before. They used their beauty to move mad weight.

Damien stopped looking out the window, finished his meal paid the bill and left Mama Mia's. He headed to one of his stash houses to meet his cousin Mike to collect money and re-up his order.

At the stash spot, he plopped down in a chair and surfed through the TV channels. He put something he liked on and leaned back, shutting his eyes to think for a moment. Mrs. Kelley interrupted his thoughts. She and her husband lived in the stash spot. Mr. Kelley was a hustler from the old school, now long since retired from the Game.

They rarely left the house and only had a few visitors, so it was perfect. Mrs. Kelley asked Damien if he wanted anything to eat or drink while she was in the kitchen.

"Naw," Damien said. "I ate at Mama Mia's."

"Oh, alright," Mrs. Kelley said, sounding disappointed. "But you're still a growing young man, Damien."

She had already conspired to cut Damien a piece of banana cream pie, which she knew he couldn't resist. Teenage boys were always hungry, whether they admitted it or not. Besides, she knew it was Damien's favorite.

Mrs. Kelley brought Damien his dessert, along with a drink. Damien smiled at his old friend. Mrs. Kelley could never take no for an answer. Since Damien already ate lunch, he knew she would come up with some kind of dessert, so he made sure he didn't have any at the restaurant.

"Thank you, Mrs. K.," Damien said, after he was done eating. "That was good, as always."

"Anytime, Damien. You're always welcome."

"Mrs. K., I'll be downstairs, alright?"

"Okay, hun."

He went down to the finished basement, where there was pool table and not much else, except some chairs and a built-in bookcase, and his safe that stood next to the bookcase in front of an exposed concrete wall. He stood in front of the safe, removed a key fob from his pocket and depressed the button. The concrete wall slid behind the built-in bookcase. All smoke and mirrors. The Kelley's knew Damien stashed stuff there, but thought it was all in the safe. In truth, the safe only held close to a hundred grand in cash.

Kain owned the building, which was a duplex, and the both of them installed the hidden room. Only Kain and Damien knew of its existence. There was another hidden door on the opposite side, leading to the other side of the duplex just in case they needed to use it in an emergency.

Damien had known the Kelley's since his days when he visited his pops on the weekends. They lived down the street on the Court. Damien would listen to Mr. Kelley's stories about his life while they smoked up. When the Kelley's were looking for a place to move into, Damien had told them about this place. They were trustworthy people, who let Damien keep work and cash in the safe.

The stash spot was Damien's largest, although he had others. Most of his product was stored there, and it was the only stash spot that held artillery.

He entered the room and depressed the button once more to close the hermetically-sealed door behind him. He put the fob back into his pocket and picked up a remote. He used it to turn on a 42" flat panel TV. Displayed on its divided screen were all the views from the concealed cameras around both units of the duplex and its property.

Damien took nothing for granted. He knew nobody knew about the stash spot, but he liked to see what was going on above him, always being cautious. However, no one would come down while he was in the "safe." Mr. Kelley would sometimes shout down to him, and he would yell up to him to come down, but that rarely happened.

Damien went right to work putting together his orders. When he got done filling them, he looked at his Movado Valor and was surprised he had been there for two hours. He picked up the two duffel bags he filled and went out the concealed door, secured it, and went upstairs.

He brought the bags out to his car that was parked in the garage connected to the duplex. After putting the heavy-ass bags onto the back seat, he went back into the house.

Mrs. Kelley told him that her husband would be upset that he didn't get a chance to see him. "Ya know he likes your company?"

"I'll be back in a few days and hopefully I'll get to see him then." He gave Mrs. K. a big hug, before handing her an envelope containing several thousand dollars. The rent he paid them for letting him keep the safe in their home. He paid them well, because he liked them a lot and knew they could use the money.

After saying his goodbyes, Damien got into his car and went to his place to drop off one of the bags at his stash spot. He then headed to meet his cousin Mike. Damien just hoped he wasn't late as usual. He was carrying way more weight than he would have liked. *He better be on time.*

The mall parking lot was packed, which was how Damien liked it. He waited, in his car, for his cousin, and he was getting nervous because he was late. Damien decided to wait inside Panera Bread, because its floor to ceiling windows allowed him to watch the parking lot for his cousin and keep an eye on his car.

Damien sat at a table eating a chicken sandwich and a broccoli-and-cheddar soup in a sourdough bread bowl. As he ate, he kept a watchful eye on his car while waiting for Mike. He saw the car that he knew his cousin would be driving pull in and park next to the rental Damien had driven there.

His cousin came inside, ordered a sandwich and a coffee, and then went over to sit with Damien. Mike put down the Macy's bag he was carrying. Clothing peeked out the top. Underneath the clothes were two shoe boxes filled with money. Damien checked the bag's contents, as his cousin picked up his food order and came back. Satisfied for now, for the money still needed to be counted, Damien swapped car keys with Mike.

They ate and talked idly about whatever came up.

"Yo, cuz, what's ya doin today?"

"Nothin," Damien replied, thinking about the other moves he needed to make before going to the store to work.

"Yo, cuz, how many you sleeve me?"

"Ten on top, so twenty altogether."

"Alright, sounds good to me."

They finished eating and went to their cars. He in Mike's rental and Mike in his. Damien drove to his crib and dropped off the money at the apartment downstairs from his. He picked up the other bag that he had dropped off there earlier and went up to his crib.

Damien's people met him, and dropped off their money, then either came back later or met him somewhere else to pick up their supply. Those who came by would hang out for a while before they hit the streets to go back to work. *Flippin them brickz.*

Chapter Fourteen

Time always seemed to escape Damien, as a few more weeks blinked passed him. Within a months time the landscape of crews trying to make money on the same streets changed. New crews popped up, from various cities and towns, including Da Bean, and they all came like it was a modern-day gold rush.

The onslaught of new crews didn't hurt Da W8 Movaz, because they were on another level. However, Crazy E didn't like it because he was beyond greedy. A large reason for his greed was that he needed to recoup the losses of losing *his* major customers, who defected back to Jimmy, after they heard he was home. Damien wasn't sure, despite Crazy E's assurances. "I'm okay with them scrams, anyhow. Buster's always complained and shit, fuck 'em, their loss." Damien wasn't so sure though, something just didn't feel right. The problem was you just didn't know when it came to Crazy E. He'd say one thing and do another.

Most of the crews were respectful, but Da Brickz started to get too small for some of them and they started fighting over territory. The Da Brickz started to get a bit too hot.

The Outside Boyz had been in town for about a year. They caused their share of the problems, because they were just like Crazy E and his Crazy 8s. They both had that clap 'em up gangsta attitude. An attitude Damien despised for war brought heat, cops, and fewer customers. Crazy's crew always seemed to be bangin with them, which made zero sense to Damien, because Crazy E made more money than the Outside Boyz' whole crew.

Crazy 8s and the Outside Boyz were bringing drama wherever they went, with straight disregard for anyone. They had no respect for any person, crew, or place. They would war no matter where they were. The leader of the Outside Boyz was a cat named Tito, who thought that "being all about it" would bring his crew business. He was wrong. The cats were small-timing in the worst way, which made Crazy E's involvement seem even worse. Da W8 Movaz were Ballers in these damned Brickz.

Legit flags also took up residence in Da Brickz; however, there were a lot of youngins flagged up on the block. There were red and blue flags everywhere. Most were scrams. They held no knowledge or heat. There were some thorough cats and about it, for real. But mostly these cats just hung out, just chillin.

After Kain moved away from the block, it seemed like no one cared about Da Brickz anymore. Damien, always loyal, tried to show Kain respect every time he chilled on the block, which he still did on some weekends. Everyone on Damien's block knew he was the manager of Da Urban Clothing Store at the mall, but they didn't know that he moved shit on the street. Damien's crew was notorious, although, most people didn't know who ran it. They assumed Crazy E did for a while, but he since had his Crazy 8s Crew, people stopped thinking it was him. Although a lot of people remember Damien selling weed back in the day, most believed that Kain got him off the streets.

The new cats drove Damien crazier than Crazy E did, for they believed that they had to be thug to clock on their block. Damien had to get violent a few times to get the job done, but it was never the first option, and he would never do something without first thinking it through.

"Do it right, or not at all," Kain would say.

Damien planned to go on vacation in two weeks, but the new drama made him be cautious. Maybe he would go just for a week to see how Jimmy would handle things, and if that worked out he'd take Kim on that month-long tour of the Caribbean he promised her. He also knew that since summer was coming business would pick up. It always did in the summertime. Party central. There were about 30 more days until summer hit. Damien talked himself into taking Kim on a week-long vacation in Aruba.

Kim and Damien already had their passports and made sure everything was in order so they could leave. Fights, hotels, and transportation booked.

Since he could do it, Damien believed anyone could, so Jimmy should have no problem.

$

The morning came for them to leave. The limo came at 10 AM; the chauffeur put their luggage in the trunk of the limo.

"Mind the store. We'll be back in a week."

"I got this, come on, get going."

"Okay, okay," Damien said, smiling before he climbed into the limo.

Jimmy watched as the limo pulled away from the curb and disappeared down the street. He had been ready for this day for two weeks. Damien sat back and had him doing all the moves. Jimmy foresaw no real problems. He figured all he had to do is what he had been doing.

The only thing he didn't look forward to was dealing with Crazy E. Damien may be in denial, but Jimmy was well aware of Crazy E's resentment towards him. He hoped Crazy E didn't try pulling any stupid shit. Jimmy thought it was obvious that Crazy E believed he should be the one handling things for Damien. Unfortunately, Damien needed this vacation and hopefully would see things more clearly when he got back.

Damien was right. The job was easy. It wasn't like it had been before Jimmy got locked. All he had to do was drop off and pick up. No more grindin hard to move product, at least on Damien's side of the business. What needed to be done could be done by anyone. Even dumb-ass Crazy E. Jimmy's cell went off, vibrating in his pocket. He pulled it out to check the screen.

"Huh…think about the devil," Jimmy mumbled before answering the call. "What's poppin C?"

"Nothin at all, my man. Did our boy leave?"

"Sure did. Just watched them drive off."

"Good, hope they has a good time," Crazy E said. "I needs to see you."

"Aight, sounds good. The usual?"

"Nah, dawg, I needs five more, and I'm not picking up what we had in common."

"Got it, when do you want to meet?"

"How bout an hour?"

"Yeah, I can do that," Jimmy said, "so fifteen, right, just that?"

"Yuh, nigga. See you then, one."

"Yeah, one."

He already had stuff in an apartment no one knew about-his stash spot, where an old man name Luis lived. The Old man kept to himself. Work then home. Same routine for 30 years. The perfect place.

$

Walking to his car, Crazy E thought about his plans for the day, and the thing he had in the works. He would meet up with this motherfucker and drop off the dough. Then his team would do this thing of theirs. He decided to drop the weed after he lost the 30-pound play back to Jimmy. It made him realize it wasn't worth his time. Jimmy probably needed it way more than he did anyway. He was movin ten brickz a week and just upped to fifteen. He was about to blow the fuck up.

His own crew, the Crazy 8s, were movin mad product to everyone they could. Although he smashed the fuck out of it, his customers still were loving the product. Shit, the motherfuckers were still getting fishscale, no matter what. Lazy-ass motherfuckers like Jon Jon, who dipped on them could have made a killin if he did the same, but that cat just wanted to move product without doing shit while getting a good price, even if the stuff was straight garbage.

Crazy E knew the clown's new connect. He had chilled with him at the Foxy Lady. Homeboy's product was barely stronger, if at all, than his own— after he cut it. *Fuck that cat; Jon Jon was lucky Damien said not to nod his bitch-ass.*

Once he made this move with his man, Blood, he and his crew would be on top. As far as he was concerned, Da W8 Movaz' were on their own. He had a new team now. All he cared about at the moment was their product, because it was fish all day. But he decided that if they don't give him the respect he deserves than they could get too.

Damien was always telling him what he could or couldn't do, "Don't war with them Outside Boyz or the bangers, no matter what color they rock" or "whatever the problem is, you need to just chill;" "You're making the block hot, dawg;" "You need to stop clappin your shit off, chill." Who did Damien think he was? Shit, Kain's boy, so what. The big guy didn't matter anymore. Did Damien think he was soft or something? Crazy E always looked at like this: If you disrespect him, he would lay you the fuck down, *plain and simple.*

If his plans with Blood went right, he'd double his order in three days. He would then sell the stomped, rerocked bricks for between twenty-two and twenty-three thousand. They couldn't get enough. Blood was willing to pay twenty-four, because that was the price he was paying. He no longer cared who ran Damien's crew, as long as he got his.

Chapter Fifteen

Damien and Kim arrived in Aruba and got to their hotel early in the evening. The room was spacious and overlooked the Caribbean Sea. They went out to dinner, then to a casino and finished the night at a club.

Morning came hard and fast. They were laying out in the sun, on their second day, soaking up the rays, which was what Kim wanted to do. The beach was semi-private, but there were still tanned and not-so-tanned bodies all around them

The posh resort was paradise with its views of the crystal-clear, blue-green waters of the Caribbean. It was like nothing he ever saw. Damien thought the other tourists would look down on them because of the way they dressed, him with his baggy clothes and all the ice they both wore. They stayed flossin.

Damien was with the most beautiful woman he had ever seen. *Kim was his world,* he thought before getting back to the book he brought. He only had 30 pages left. He could not believe he had read 165 pages within the past two hours. So far Damien really liked the novel, which was written by Teri Woods. She was real, and he like that she wrote about Da Brickz. He couldn't wait to read her next one.

The books were given to him by Jimmy, who read them while he was in the county. Jimmy told him he would like them, and so far he did. He was already set to read the sequel: Dutch 2. Damien had never heard of street books or urban fiction before he got these, but now he was definitely a fan of the genre. The way Jimmy told it urban fiction novels were sought-after reading materials inside. Damien finished the book and wondered if anyone would write about their Brickz. *Only if Crazy E was more like Craze. That man was loyal to the fullest.*

It was a great day. Damien had taken kim to all the little shops, and they had a good-time just being together. They ended the day with dinner at the blue Lagoon, where they had reservations. He called Jimmy to check on things back home.

Jimmy assured him everything was good, and he told him that he met up with Crazy E.

"I met him bout an hour after you left, and he added five more and dropped our common commodity."

"About time he decided to make money," Damien said then gave him the number to the hotel room just in case he needed him for any reason.

Whitney called earlier to make sure they had arrived safely and that they were good. They had good friends who truly cared about them. It seemed that things would be okay. He would be home in a few days anyway.

Knowing things were good back home allowed him to relax and focus on Kim. She was more than special, maybe even perfect. She was down to ride or die and unlike his boys' girlfriends who always seemed to bring some kind of drama, it never happened with Kim. Sure they argued but it was never over something petty. They had known each other since they were eleven years old. Seven years later they were together and had been for about three years. Who knew what would be in their future.

After dinner, they went back to the hotel to get ready to go out to a club. However, Kim had other plans. As Damien lay on the bed listening to the street music coming in through the open patio doors, Kim came dancing out of the bathroom wearing only her lingerie.

She was stunning, with a curvy body that fit her 5' 4" frame. Kim turned him on as she danced seductively, undulating her belly back and forth while spinning around to the rhythm of the festive music outside.

The three pieces of laced clothing that covered her knockout figure started to slowly come off. With graceful rhythmic movements, her hips swayed, oh so, slowly side to side, back and forth, as she removed her see-through top. She started swinging it overhead, around her fingers, doing her own strip tease.

She tossed the top in Damien's face, as the slow rhythm carried her closer to him. She expertly spun around to the succession of the drums and on the final beat her brassiere flew over Damien's head, exposing her cantaloupe-sized breasts that were now free to bounce to their own rhythm, which excited Damien more.

He grew rock-hard with anticipation for what was to come from such an unplanned act. It was far more exciting than he could ever explain. She danced as close to him as possible without touching him. She stood swaying her figure to the music and reached out, clasping her hands behind his neck and pulling him forward into her chest.

He buried his face in her breasts, kissing and sucking on each one, as softly as he could. Kim pushed him backwards onto the bed, while climbing on top of him. She exposed his throbbing member, and fondled him, making it even harder than he thought possible. She moved her G-string to one side and positioned herself on the head of his cock, barely allowing the tip to go in, teasing him, making him want it even more.

His hardened cock entered her warm, wet pussy, as she began to ride him up and down, moving her hips and working it, as her ripe melons were once again being enjoyed by his passionate tongue. Kim was pushing Damien to his limit. After several minutes, they changed position, her legs were now up in the air, with her ass barely on the bed, as he took control.

He entered her with raw passion, as he thrust his cock in and out of her, slowly at first until they were at a gallop. As the beat gained tempo, he went faster. Kim was panting and moaning, as she belted out, "Baby deeper…push it…oh, baby…work it!" Their passionate love making went on for two hours. Afterwards, they headed down to the beach, where their lovemaking continued.

Chapter Sixteen

On the Cape and the islands, Damien's boy Roc had things locked down in the skin trade. Rich dudes loved to be escorted by straight dimes, whether they were ghetto or not. They wanted the best and got it. Roc's girls would do anything for him. They all loved him and made money the way they chose. Roc wasn't a pimp in the original sense, no he was just a straight pimp, in the new sense. He had 50 girls and over the few years he ran his escort service, many girls left to do their own thing or just got out the Game.

His girls old and new would provide Roc with everything that the tricks told them, whether it seemed important or not, letting Roc decide. He had his girls' trickin some of the top players around, including prominent businessmen and politicians. Roc had dirt on a lot of people. Roc learned through one of his girls, Amanda, that Tito was planning some kind of raid to push Crazy E off the block. A hostile takeover with guns.

Crazy E stayed on the block 24/7, the only W8 Mova who did, letting his business be known. Matters were exacerbated by the impression that

Crazy E ran Da W8 Movaz, and the Crazy 8s were their army. The other 8 members of Da W8 Movaz, unlike Crazy E, moved on the low. They were invisible to the casual onlooker.

According to Amanda, Tito thought if he took out some of the crew it would weaken Da W8 Movaz' hold on the streets, but if he could get Crazy E, himself, it would be the end of Da W8 Movaz altogether.

Roc wasn't sure whether Amanda had it right or not, but they seemed to be targeting Crazy E and his crew. As far as he was concerned, Crazy E brought it on himself, but Damien and the rest of Da W8 Movaz were a different story. Damien had been his boy for seven years, and it was Dee who lent him the cash to start his Roc-a-Babe escort service. When Amanda first told him, he was just gonna let it happen, but not doing something could get his friends hurt. He may not like Crazy E, but the rest of the crew was fam.

According to Amanda, she overheard Tito talking on the phone to some cat named Jon Jon, but she wasn't sure. He just hoped it wasn't the same Jon Jon that used to be down with the crew.

He figured that the Outsiders would run-up on the block in about a week. She kept it real by telling him. That's Daddy's girls—loyal. She thought he would want to know, because she knew he fucked with them W8 Movaz.

Roc knew what needed to be done. Damien always kept it 100. The cat helped him out with his business and any drama that came his way. *Fuck them niggas up, dawg, fam is fam.*

$

Tito was chillin at his sister's crib at the Heights, a housing development that had several buildings totaling 200 apartments or more. It was ghetto. When his sister moved down here, he thought that she was on the come-up, for real, but section 8 is what it is everywhere. He still was amazed at how much money could be made in the complex.

He eventually saw that there was more money to be made outside of the complex and started having his people move down to the Brickz. They hustled hard, taking no shorts. They were outsiders in town, and people started calling them the Outside Boyz. It was what they were, so they didn't see anything wrong with the name. As a matter of fact, they liked it because it represented them perfectly.

Tito saw that this cat Crazy E was caking it up on the Ave. The cat was a lot like him in many ways, but would never give him the time of day. When Tito first moved down, he tried to get on through Crazy E, but the cat took it to another level, "Sorry, dawg, but I don't fuck with no broke niggas and ain't going to start either."

Tito wanted to blast him then, for the blatant dis-respect, but knew it would have done no good and got him nowhere real fast. Instead, he got his grind on by himself until he was able to bring his team in. They weren't the Crazy 8s, nor Da W8 Movaz, but they made their money. Although, he knew that Crazy E would see them as broke-ass crumb snatchers, but that was all about to change.

The way Tito saw it was Crazy E that had everything to lose and he didn't. They were going to take Crazy E's crew out. Many people hated Crazy E, so it was easy to recruit people to be down with his team. Tito also heard that the manager of the Urban Clothing Store at the mall used to run with Da W8 Movaz—even helped start it—but Crazy E fucked shit up and dude got out of the Game.

Every weekend Crazy E chilled outside on the Ave, on the same stoop he chilled on since he had been a kid. Tito planned to have cats all over the Ave. Ready to nod any motherfucker that's with him. Crazy E and his soldiers were always together, unless they were making moves up and down the Ave.

Tito also knew that there was a serious cat whom lived over there that everyone respected. However, he recently heard that the cat moved to some big-ass house somewhere else in town. *So, he hoped.* As long as the baller was gone, he saw no problem. *None.*

Chapter Seventeen

The week was going smooth; Jimmy couldn't believe how peaceful it had. Jimmy sat at his workstation, in the room he rented off the old man, putting together an order for most of the team. Everyone suddenly needed a lot of shit. Damien explained that when he touched down that he was movin a few birds, but the truth was closer to 40 birds a week. The money Jimmy was seeing pass through his hands was enormous, as well as corrupting. This was *Paid in full* type of money. He now understood why Dee put him in charge. *Crazy's dumb-ass would've got greedy enough to pull a Rico move.*

Jimmy couldn't believe that Crazy E had called him yesterday for the same order as before. Damn, fifteen birds flying out the coup in two days was insane. Then Whitney called this morning to double their order. Double! Mind blowing. How do you double up on twelve keys? Now it was twenty-four. Of course, it was just beginning, Julio needed ten more for him and Dez. What the fuck! Jimmy knew he didn't have that on hand, so he would have to go to Damien's stash. The twenty he had for the week was already gone.

He grabbed a duffel bag and went over to Damien's, first stopping to check on Damien's apartment, before heading to the spot he kept in the building. The safe was big but he hoped there would be enough to at least fill the orders. That way he could relax for the rest of the week until Damien got back. Although Jimmy had been making moves for Damien, he had never seen this safe, never mind what was inside. Damien had warned him that because summer was coming that he may run out, and if that happened what was in there would bail him out.

He doubted it would because he needed twenty more just to complete the total order. How much could he possibly have? Jimmy entered the number: 3-7-3-5-5-7 into the keypad. The screen prompted him to enter the second password: 3-4-7-4-7-2-2-5-3.

He hoped it was the right code. In an instant, he got his answer: password accepted. The safes elaborate password protection provided an extra layer of security in case someone figured out the first pass code. Damien was slick, Jimmy thought, because the total password stated: D-SELLS-FISHSCALE.

He cracked open the heavy door. What Jimmy saw inside made him blink. He had to look twice. Damn, there had to be at least 50 fuckin bricks in the safe. Jimmy took double what he needed and went back to his crib…in shock. He knew his man was doin it big, but what the fuck. Why didn't he tell him? Where did it all come from? Of course, he knew that it came from Kain, but damn, that was a lot of powder.

Jimmy looked side to side and all around, as he carried the heavy burden back to the stash spot. He couldn't believe he was just lugged that shit back without a burner. He began to finish the order. As he did that, he thought about all the other shit the team wanted, and felt as though he was gonna pass out, but instead he told them the 100-pounds of weed and thousands of pills they each needed had to wait. *Damn, they were ballin.*

Dez knew that shit just seemed too damn good. The streets had them and the Game wasn't about to let the go. The Game never let anyone go until it was through with them. Unfortunately, when it did, it wasn't always to retire healthy and old. Prison or death was more often the Game's choice in terminating the relationship.

Dez and Julio's shop was doing real good. Hustlers from across the state told their boys that Coastal Customs was the place to get your ride hooked up. A select few knew that Dez could install self-contained, hermetically sealed hides in their rides. The hides that dez installed didn't use hydraulics nor were they connected to the fuse box, so they were virtually invisible. Some of his hides were disguised as working items that could be found in a car or home. *Wasn't technology great.*

"Do things right or not at all," Damien had told them a hundred times. His stash boxes were legendary. If you were a serious hustler, you wanted one. You may not know where to get one, but if you were a baller, you knew someone who could point you in the right direction.

Dez, laughed at himself, because he never admitted to doing them, but he'd tell people he knew a guy. The whole team had them and the way Jimmy was acting on the phone it would seem they were needed.

He finished up a custom-dropped Escalade. Dez had to install a 42" LCD TV in the truck, and it would be complete. The TV would be held in an enclosure directly behind the front seats. The motorized enclosure enabled the TV to come out of its hiding place to be viewed, while also acting as a partition — separating the front from the back.

The truck looked nothing as it originally did, with its custom paint, body, and interior. The truck was smokin. It put almost any of the rides in those magazines to shame. It was one of their best jobs and sure to bring them more business. As he finished up installing the LCD TV, his cell erupted, with Fat Joe rappin," Dust your shoulders off." He picked up the cell, answering it without checking to see who it was. "What's good?"

"Everything went smooth," Julio said. "I'll be there in like twenty minutes, aight dawg?

"That's cool, see you then," Dez said, then hung up before dialing another number. He waited for the beep then said, "Your truck's ready. Come pick it up. Aight, Mike, I'll check you out later."

What a day, Dez mused. First he finished a truck that the owner had put more than 40 stacks into, and second Julio just picked up 10 birds that will produce closer to 20 when they're done: Chop, rerock, and move. *Life was good.*

$

Miguel could not believe his eyes, but the money before him displayed the truth. The five keys he picked up should have held him over until next week, but it didn't.

"Diablo!" He whispered to himself, realizing that he just went through seven birds, because he had two when Damien dropped off the rest. His man had straight fishscale, so he made a killin, but he felt nervous with all that cash at his stash spot.

He was stompin his competition, never mind the product. There were now six members on his team. Most of the crew were made up of friends Miguel and Damien grew up with. Miguel was quiet about doing The-damn-thing, so no one he didn't want to know didn't.

He was a ghost.

"Live and maintain," he said to himself, just like his favorite movie. He couldn't wait until Damien got back because he already needed to see him, again. *Life in the Game.*

Whitney counted their money, so she could make a drop to Kim's man. She and Kim ran the Dime Pack, and they had eight weight customers and were about to stop fuckin with anything smaller than a bird. Twenty-four birds in one week was crazy, but it's what they did. It had taken them a few years to get to this level. *But damn, twenty-four!*

They knew motherfuckers who had been in the Game for ten, fifteen years, and still stacked minor figures. Of course, there were also cats doing a 10 to 15 year stretch courtesy of the Game. She knew that if it wasn't for Damien, and his connect, they would have to grind hard just to stack minor figures, themselves. Nobody else would have taken a chance with a bunch of young-ass kids the way Damien did. Damien had a serious connect, which made it easy for them to move mad-product. *Endless opportunities.*

Chapter Eighteen

Jimmy tried to get ahold of Damien at the hotel. He called several times already and decided to give it one more shot.

The phone rang. "Hello," an exhausted female voice inquired.

"What's good, baby girl?" Jimmy said recognizing Kim's voice. "Where tha man at?"

"He's right here, Jimmy. Hold on," Kim said, as she called to Damien, letting him know Jimmy was on the phone. "He'll be right here, Jimmy. How are you, is everything good?"

"I'm not sure yet. It might be nothing," he said, not believing himself. "That's why I need to talk to Dee."

"Well, here he is, I'll talk to you later."

"What's up, dawg?" Damien said. "Everything aight?"

"Nah, dawg…we may have a problem."

"What is it, I'm listening."

"Well, Roc called me after he kept getting your voicemail."

"Yeah, go on."

"He said that the Outside Boyz are gonna run-up on the block."

"What? Did he say why?"

"Yeah, dawg, I guess these cats are gonna run through the block clappin and shit, 'cause theys think Crazy E runs shit, you heard?"

"Yeah, man, go on, is there anything else?"

"This muthafucka named Tito thinks that we all work for Crazy E, so some of us are in his sights too."

"Who?"

"Don't know. Roc only told me to stay off the block."

"Sounds like good advice, but what do you think?"

"Well, I don't know. Maybe we need to fallback a little until we get more information. You never know, it might be just talk."

"It could be, but I doubt it. I say that because Roc called us. If he thinks it's serious, then we should listen."

"True."

"Want me to come home? We'll be on the next flight. Your call."

"Nah, kid, enjoy your vacation. You'll be home in a couple days anyways. But Dee, there is one thing that's for certain."

"What's that?"

"Crazy E is fuckin up our shit…. and he's putting us in danger. Why do the Outside Boyz have beef wit him, or us, anyhow?"

"I don't know, not for sure, anyway, but I remember when Tito first came to town he was straight broke. He didn't have any money until later. Crazy E told me some shit about Tito, but that shit was before the Outside Boyz got their name, so your guess is as good as mines."

"I have no clue, either. But Crazy E hasn't been a fan of mines since I got back."

"Well, I'll have to think about this one, but see if Roc can find out more, and keep everyone off the block, including Crazy E, but don't tell him why, 'cause he'll cause mad drama."

"I got it, dawg, one."

"One."

They both hung up wondering what was going on.

Unaware to either the Outside Boyz nor the Da W8 Movaz, the Red Rags were also planning to do a drive-by on the same block at the same time because two high ranking Blue Rags just moved to the corner near the stoop. They would hang outside on the corner for hours, very visible. It was yards away from the same stoop that Crazy E is known to chill, especially on the weekends.

The reds were gunnin for them in retaliation for them shooting up there spot a few weeks before. All-out war was about to erupt in Da Brickz. Forget about Iraq; the war was coming home.

Chapter Nineteen

Jimmy left several messages on everyone's voice-mail, asking them to call him ASAP. According to Roc, shit was going down sometime in the near future, and no one answered their damn cells.

He finally got ahold of Ty, who was on his way to make a move in Brockton.

"Call me when you're back in the area, alright?"

"No problem…everything good?"

"Things are *crazy*, and I need everyone to swing by, so if you hear from anyone, pass it along."

Ty knew something was up, but he agreed to come through when he got back, and pass along Jimmy's message. He also told Jimmy that he needed another bird. *Damn, these things were flying out the coop.*

Jimmy had to go to the store to work, but his mind stayed on the drama about to go down. Anyone looking at Jimmy would be able to tell something was wrong. You could see the worry engraved into his face.

Christy noticed immediately that something was wrong. "Everything alright? You don't look too good."

"Yeah, I'm okay, just not feeling right today." Since the day they met, she showed concern for him.

They had gone out a few times. He could hardly believe that it had only been a month. *Damn, that's all it's been, seemed like forever ago.*

He watched her, as she went back to straighten a stack of clothes on a low table. He tried his best to keep her sheltered from the hustling side of his life. Things were good, and he was trying to keep them that way.

Jimmy was helping a customer when Julio and Dez walked through the doors. They were rarely ever seen together anymore. He finished with the customer. *They must be done for the day.*

Julio gave Jimmy dap, so did Dez, "What's up… you guys good?

"Us," Julio said, "damn, you the one who hit Dez and me up like sixty times, and shit."

"Yeah, we good," Dez interjected, "but what's up with you?"

"I need to talk to the whole team."

"Well, we talked to Ty and he talked to Whit, and everyone's gonna swing through here."

"Perfect," he said. It was music to his ears, because it meant nobody would be on the block.

"We even told Crazy E," Julio said.

"But he said he gots too much shit to do on the block, then worry about some fuckin meetin and shit, like we a fuckin company or some shit."

"That was a direct quote from him too," Julio said.

Jimmy shook his head. *What a dumbass. Fuck it, though, it's his life.*

Chapter Twenty

Jimmy was glad that Crazy E's dumbass didn't come. Now, he could tell everyone what was going down. He couldn't have done that with Crazy E present. They gathered in the Break Room, which was a perfect spot for a meeting like this. Jimmy, thanks to Roc, had found out exactly what was going down over the weekend. *He wondered if he should call Damien.*

The crew waited in silence for Jimmy to begin and wondered why Roc was there. The team hadn't been in one place since his coming home party. It was good to see everyone, but he wished it was under a different set of circumstances. Jimmy didn't want to accidentally leave something out or plain get it wrong, so he had Roc come to tell everyone himself.

"Okay, what's this about?" Whitney said.

"Yeah, what's so important, is our boy okay?" Dez added, as everyone tried to speak at once.

Jimmy calmed everyone down, so he could speak. "Look, there's a lot goin on, and it has nothing to do with you all right here."

"What chu mean?" Julio asked.

"We have reason to believe that the Outside Boyz are going to light up the block over the weekend. We rarely make moves from there, but we still chill on the stoop from time to time. And four of us still live there on the block, so I hope you all see our concern?"

"Why would they do that shit, and where's Crazy E?" Ty threw into the pot, "Shouldn't he be here?"

"We'll get to that, so hold on. I learned this from Roc, and that's why he's here. I'll let him explain the what, where, and how."

Roc explained everything to them, including how Tito's mistaken belief that Crazy E ran the team put them in danger. They now understood that the Outside Boyz were going to try to take out Crazy E along with those who were around him.

"Thanks Roc, that's peace," Dez said.

"Yeah thanks, but what bout Crazy E. Like Ty said, shouldn't that motherfucka be here?" Desaun said, who had moved away but was still part of the team and felt it was disrespectful to everyone that Crazy E didn't show.

"'Cause," Dez said, "he think whens we calls a meeting that he don't need to be here."

"Hold up, I'm glad that he didn't come," Jimmy said, "because if he had I wouldn't have been able to tell you all what the deal was. If Crazy E knew what the Outsiders were planning, he would retaliate, causing even more drama for us. So just in case, if anyone sees him, just tell him that we heard through Roc that the blocks hot and that the D-boys are gonna raid the block, trying to catch us slippin, aight?"

Everyone agreed to be ghost and not go near the block. Kim and Damien were away, so they were safe. Jimmy had to worry only about Ty and himself. Ty said he'd take off in the morning. Crazy E lived in the neighborhood and hung out on the block, but as far as Jimmy was concerned Crazy E brought this on himself.

Chapter Twenty-one

Kain stood on his private beach staring out to the ocean in deep thought. *Dilemmas*, he thought. It seemed to him that life was a series of dilemmas that either led to failure or success. He agreed with, Stanley I. Mason, the creator of Pyrex, who said: "If you're not succeeding enough, you're not failing enough."

Ironically, failing wasn't his problem at all. He was succeeding—thriving—faster than he had ever imagined. Of course, some of his stores weren't doing as good as others, but that was the nature of specialty retail. Under performing stores were a fact of doing business. It was difficult to know your product, customers, and competition. Unfortunately, these were the three things that presented dilemmas and created success.

Kain knew that success meant staying ahead of the curve and knowing better than the competition. For instance, in 2005, most city malls had many hip-hop clothing stores, but suburban malls had very few options, and none in exurban areas. Unlike other clothing companies, Kain did not fade hip-hop products out. He knew that his customers, those who like hip-hop gear, were everywhere, whether it was the city, suburbia, or exurbia. It one of the reasons his stores prospered. Fast-forward to 2012 and his stores not only survived the Downturn of 2008, but flourished. He had come out the other side in a changing landscape that had destroyed other specialty retailers.

Unfortunately for Kain, he had to have every store bring in enough traffic, in order for him to clean the huge amounts of cash that his other business now took in. He had to open stores near his competition to create a competitive environment that gave his customers a choice. The stores were always stocked with the latest fashions from the top brands, including his own. Despite being more than worth it, the money laundering was a pain in the ass, never mind tiring.

He admired the beautiful day, as the ocean water crashed onto the shore, sending a mild breeze in his direction. This was the life. Hard to believe this was part of the same town where he grew up. He, like Damien, moved here as a kid. It's why he helped out Dee in the first place. They had a lot in common and since no one gave him a chance to be something else, he felt he owed it to Damien. The way he helped Dee may be unorthodox, but Kain at least tried. *Just hope it was good enough.*

He tried to show Damien that money could be made in a myriad of ways without the Game. Unfortunately, Kain's lessons never seemed to convince him to stop.

Kain hoped, since the beginning, that one day he would realize he didn't need the Game. Kain would give Dee whatever he needed, but Damien's character would not allow it. Damien needed to earn his own money, both in the Game and at the store. No hand-outs. Damien's store out performed most of the other stores in the company. High earnings and very little shrinkage. He worked hard and this gave Kain hope.

Kain missed the old neighborhood, so much so, he decided to swing through. It was Friday and he didn't have to work, which made it a perfect day to checkup on the Da Brickz. Kain loved it when he drove the Lambo through. Everyone, especially the kids, acted all dumb, while at the same time it would inspire hope. Unfortunately, he was a street legend who despite his pending retirement from the Game, was in it for a long time. The wrong message could also be easily taken instead: *hustle hard and get rich.*

He didn't like the disrespect these new cats showed the block. They simply made shit hot worth their clappin and shit. He loved the small town vibe but didn't like what he believed was to be its future. Kain envisioned that the rich would move back to Boston, causing rent to be impossible to afford, and gentrification would push the ghettos deep into the suburbs. Because of the disrespect shown to the block, Kain drove through more often. Although Kain was still respected on the streets, he didn't believe his presence helped much at all. He made his plans while walking back to the house.

Chapter Twenty-two

Friday morning, at the same time Kain walked out to the beach, Tito decide it was the day. He called his people and they called theirs, and so on. He had convinced his top men to be part of the three cars that would set it off. Tito would lead them from the first car. The plan was simply to pull up and unload. They had another 20 cats committed to run up on the block on foot if needed.

Those on standby would be waiting at the top of the hill behind the apartment buildings near the stoop. Also, one car would pull up the driveway that goes behind the stoop. Ready to catch anyone running for cover. They would get hit by surprise in their own hood. *Fuck 'em*. It would be their Brickz now. The minute Crazy E's spotted chillin with enough of his crew, it's over.

$

Unbeknown to the Outside boyz, the Reds were loading up two cars that were going to light up the Blue's house. Payback for a drive-by they had done weeks prior. The consensus of the whole crew was fuck them and everyone around there; they could all get it. The leader Troy was down to get some fuckin getback. *Time had come to show them who was gangsta, and it sure wasn't them bitch-ass cats.*

Chapter Twenty-three

Crazy E woke up over Dave and Melissa's house. It was about 6 in the morning. His head was spinning. Damn, he drank too much. He got off the couch where he had passed out and went to smoke a Newport. Ty was on the porch .

"What's up, kid?"

"Not much," Ty said, before realizing."Oh, wait, one thing though, I heard through Roc that D-boys, or some shit, were gonna run through here sometime this weekend."

"Oh, yeah? Fuckin police. Good looks," Crazy E said." Thanks for the info."

Ty said goodbye and left.

Damn, he starts early, Crazy E thought.

Crazy E finished his cigarette and went back inside to gather his things before he left. A couple of Crazy 8s were already posted up on the stoop. As Crazy E passed them, he told them he'd be back. He had to run home to shower and change. He needed a haircut too, but that could wait until later.

Kim and Damien landed at T.F. Green at about 9:30 AM They had arranged for a limo to pick them up. They agreed to cut their trip short and head home. They had to make sure everything was good with their people. Besides, they had a wonderful time and felt that they were needed back home.

The Lincoln Town Car headed to one of Damien's stash spots located across town. As a precaution, they decided to stop there to pick up some heat. The spot held mostly money and guns. Damien wasn't taking any chances and was confident that not many cats had the artillery he had. He grabbed two .40 cals with 17 round clips, two FN57s with armor piercing ammo, and two P90s that were locked and loaded. Damien hoped things were good and decided to check-in with Jimmy. He picked up one of the burner phones he bought at the airport. Kim used the other to call Whit.

Jimmy answered quickly. "Hello?"

"It's me, dawg," Damien said. "We decided to come home."

"When?" Jimmy asked, with concern. He rather they were not around while this shit went down. He just didn't want anything to happen to them.

"We'll be in town in bout an hour or so. I'll call you when I'm around," he paused sensing Jimmy's fears. "Oh, don't worry, dawg, I'm not goin to the block."

"Aight, let me get up so I can get ready?"

"Sure, but don't let anyone outside the crew know I'm home."

Jimmy got out of bed and looked out the window. The sun was already heating up, and it looked like it was gonna be a hot one, for sure. The neighborhood was already bustling with activity: children were out in the street, older cats were passing a football, and hustlers posted up and down the block. It appeared to be just another day in Da Brickz.

He hoped the dirveby would happen on another day. A rainy, crappy one where only the hustlers would dare to come out. Jimmy checked the clock on his way to the bathroom to shower. It was moments past 10 in the morning. He jumped in the shower, hoping it was gonna be a good day.

Chapter Twenty-four

It was late morning just before noon. The day unfolded as Jimmy predicted. Everyone who lived on the Ave. was outside enjoying the nice day. People were on their porches or stoops. Children were running about through the neighborhood. The block had no idea about the terror that would make this the worst day in Da Brickz' history.

A titanium colored Lamborghini swung its low body onto the block from the opposite end of the street. You could hear the stereo's bass before you ever saw the exotic whip. It had to be the only Lambo in the county at the time. Kain pulled over to the curb in front of a wooden row house, while lowering its passenger side window.

Tamika and Flip walked over to the whip from their porch. They were part of Kain's circle, but hadn't seen Kain in months. Their hustle wasn't drugs, prostitution, or extortion. Nobody on the block knew what they did. They were just regular people from Da Brickz. However, they were very good with a Hamada four-color printing press, and making cloth paper, which they had in their basement. They made paper. Whatever a baller needed. Their counterfeit money was near flawless. But it was their working passports and identity papers that were incredible. A must have in the Game.

"What's going on...my nigga?" Tamika said, smiling as flip made his way around to the driver's side, checking out the car as he went.

Flip made several facial expressions of disbelief, for it was the first time he got to see Kain's whip up close. "Nice ride, dawg. Shit, this here is tight," wishing he could get one.

"Well, what else would I whip?"

"You the man, no doubt," Tamika said, thinking Tanisha's one lucky bitch to catch a nigga like Kain. This muthafucka had it goin on. Smooth too. "I gotta get back inside before theys wreck my house and shit, be safe, you hear?" She gave him a kiss and went inside to referee the ruckus that could be heard from outside. Her youngins were ten, so everything started a fight with them boys.

"Flip, you wanna ride? I'm just cruising through, letting people know I'm still here."

"Aight, dawg," he said, before turning back towards. "Yo, Mika...I'm takin a ride wit Kain."

"Aight, baby. Don't be gone too long," she hollered back from behind the screen door, with one of her boys in tow.

Aight, let's go before she changes her mind, cuz those boys drive her crazy. Now, how do I get in?"

"Use the handle," Kain said, smiling.

Flip pulled the handle and the door automatically rose up. Lost for words Flip just shook his head and kept cheesing.

After Flip got in and secured the seatbelt, the powerful V12 propelled them forward, as they cruised to the end of the street. Kain glanced at his old building, where Damien lived now, and he saw a few of the youngin's crew. Crazy E was posted up on the stoop, as usual, with some of his boys, and that cat Ty got out of his car in some kind of hurry.

"What's up fellas?" Kain said out his window, as he rolled to a standstill for the stop sign.

"What's goin on?" Crazy E said, "Everything good?"

Ty stopped his climb up the stoop and looked back to see Kain. He waved and smiled, "What's up Kain?"

Several cars were now behind them, so Kain pulled up to the stop sign. He waited for his break in the traffic on Court Street. A car pulled onto the Ave but slowed to a stop because it could not get by Kain's Lambo. Kain saw that less than a few yards from the stoop were K.C. and Jerrell all blued up. Kain had seen them at the store at the mall but didn't know they were bangers. *Too bad. Damn this traffic.*

He saw his break and pressed down on the pedal to accelerate off the Ave. As the powerful engine pushed the car forward, all hell broke loose on the block. The sound of gun fire bouncing off the close buildings. The three cars behind him were the source. Gunfire erupted in Crazy E's direction. Kain believed hellfire had finally come to meet Crazy E. But at that very moment, the occupants of the car stopped at the corner facing him popped out of their windows and lit up the bangers on that were chillin on the corner. The events happened fast, and Kain did not believe in coincidences. He mashed the aluminum pedal, which launched them off the Ave and into traffic. Cars careered around them.

Kain turned into the church parking lot. He used the horseshoe driveway to bring him around the building back to the street, where he waited out of sight. Kain saw the car that lit up the flags pass by, as well as the three that opened-up on Damien's people. As they sped by him, Kain pulled out behind them, he hoped they were paying too much attention to their escape than to the Lamborghini. Incognito Kain was not. They turned onto Bourne Road. He saw their blinkers for them to turn left onto Standish Avenue, so he punched the gas, making it to the light up ahead in seconds. The turning lane was clear allowing him to whip his car around the corner and to the next light, which was green. He let off the gas to slow down enough to see in the only car left at the red light. Kain could see the driver and knew his name was Tito.

He pressed the gas again to accelerate up the hill, where he caught up to another car of shooters, who to his surprise turned into the gas station that contained a store, a Subway, and a Dunkin Donuts. *What balls*, Kain thought, reaching inside his stash box to grab his burner, a .40 cal. A round was already in the chamber, ready for action. Flip had his own and looked eager to use it. They pulled into the gas station. The car was parked on the side of the building. Kain drove passed them on the way to the pumps.

Flip went in to the store while Kain filled up his tank. Kain finished and went into the store to give Flip money for the gas. Kain walked around the store grabbing a drink and a snack while he watched the cats from the car. They must have worked up an appetite, because they were buying stuff from each business, but Kain knew they were just making it look like they belonged.

Flip paid for the gas and his stuff and went outside. Flip started to walk back to the car but decided to go to the pay phone on the side of the building where the shooters parked. When he got to the payphone, Flip noticed a teenager cross the parking lot from the direction of the Dumpster back to his car. Flip used the payphone to call Kain.

"Hello?"

"Yo, it's me. One of those cats just came from the Dumpster."

"Oh, yeah?"

"Yup."

"Check it out, aight, dawg?"

"Plan on it," Flip said, hanging up the phone, before walking over to the Dumpster. Flip got to it and peered inside. At first, he couldn't see anything. He glanced around making sure nobody was watching him. He looked inside finding what he was looking for—burners. He only saw three, but there were five motherfuckers in that whip. At least, two guns still remained. He threw some trash away and headed back to Kain's ride.

The rest of the shooters came out of the store. Flip saw one of them pointing at the Murcielago. Kain came out as they got into their whip and chilled. Flip made it halfway when Kain motioned for him to drive and tossed him the keys. Kain walked to the shooters car. Flip picked up the pace. He was about to get his driving wish, but it wasn't exactly what he had in mind. He secured himself behind the wheel; he saw Kain at the shooters driver's side window with his heat in his hand, against his thigh, concealed in the ruffles of his jeans.

Kain approached the driver, whose window was down. "What's up," he said, 'maybe you'll be able to help me. I've been driving around lost for the past hour, but after what I just saw, I really don't want to be around here." He pointed to his lambo, which was now headed their way. "So do you know where the Independence Mall is?"

"Yeah, it's right up the street. It will be on your left."

"Thanks," Kain said. "Oh, by the way, never shoot up my block, you dumbass bitches." Kain squeezed off five precise head shots, with his silenced .40 cal. *That's how it's down, quietly.*

Kain jumped into his whip and they headed back to the block. They took the long way home, up pass the mall, through the old plaza to North Spooner Street headed to Flip's house. They turned onto the Ave. and Blue lights lit up the neighborhood. Flip pulled into his driveway, while Kain was on the phone.

"Who?"

"No one knows for sure," Jimmy said, some say it was them Outside Boyz, but others say it was the Reds."

"What's the damage?"

"Well, dawg, they got Ty as he was walkin up the stoop to his house."

Damn, he alright?"

"I don't know; they MedFlighted him to Boston, but I heard he's critical."

"I'll make sure he gets the best doctors."

"I thought you would." Jimmy said, "They also got crazy E and five of his crew that were posted up on the stoop. Only Crazy E and one other made it."

"He survived?"

"Yeah, but that's not all."

"I never liked that cat…it figures."

"Bet the ones that got it were good people?"

"They were, also I was sayin, to make matters worse one other got shot and died instantly, but he was only fourteen-years-old, just some kid tryin to be down."

"Call our man to let him know."

"He already does. He at his crib now, guess he pulled up when it went down. He saw everything, including a nice-ass whip leaving the scene in a real hurry."

in that wondrous light. He wanted to merge with it. He wanted to become it.

Then the light met the darkness that infested his soul. Opposites collided. There was a brief, violent struggle, but the darkness was stronger. It expelled the light.

"No!" He reached out and tried to grab it, to hold on to it, but it slipped through his fingers like quicksilver. It started to fade, and he sobbed. For a brief instant in time, he had possessed something wonderful, only to have it ripped away by the darkness that was consuming him. Then, just before the light faded completely, a tiny, needle thin beam shot out. It pierced the darkness like a doctor's scalpel and sliced straight into Garrett's innermost being.

"Look at me, Dad. See me for who I really am." The woman still stood before him, her hand on his chest. The beam sank deep into Garrett's spirit, and as it did, it formed a bridge between the two of them. He looked into her eyes...

...and saw his daughter.

"Molly?" Relief flooded her face.

"Yes," Molly whispered. "It's me, but our time is almost gone." Garrett struggled to keep himself under control.

"You're...you're alive," he gasped. The implications crashed into his mind. "There's life after death. There is, isn't there?"

"Oh Dad, you have no idea," said Molly.

"Are we...do we..." Garrett could not form the words, but with the link between them, words were unnecessary.

"Everything that matters, we take with us; our memories, our feelings, our *love*. It's a long journey, but we *never* forget." Her eyes looked past him, as if she was seeing something unimaginably far away. "It's a journey that I am going to have to take soon, but not just yet. I've been given this little slice of time. I have to help you free Mom."

"Molly…" The link wavered. Garrett could feel the darkness pushing in from all sides.

"There's no time, Dad," said Molly. "He's got her, and he's not going to let her go. You're going to have to take her away from him."

"Who? Who has her?"

"He used to be John Gamble," said Molly. Again the link wavered, and for an instant Garrett was certain that it was going to wink out. Then it firmed up, although now he could see that it was only a matter of (seconds?) before the darkness destroyed it.

"Who is he?" demanded Garrett and then shook his head. "No, *where* is he? Where can I find him?"

"You have to…" The link disappeared, and Molly screamed. Suddenly, the darkness broke though the flimsy barrier Garrett had managed to erect. It smashed into the light, obliterating it.

"Molly!" He was still at the campsite, but he was now alone. NO!" For a terrible moment, he thought that his daughter had been destroyed. Then, from unimaginably far away, he heard her call out to him.

Come back to me, she cried, only now her voice barely registered in his mind. *Come back to me, and you'll find Mom.* Then the darkness overrode everything. Garrett felt his carefully constructed tunnel start to crumble. Suddenly, he was taken by something vile. It felt as if slimy tentacles, soft and yet as strong as steel, had wrapped themselves around him. With a jolt, he was dragged back through the dissolving tunnel. Then he was back in his bed, lying next to the thing that was pretending to be Molly Webb.

The pain consumed him. He curled into a fetal position and screamed. His sheets were now soaked with blood. Dimly, he wondered just how much more he could afford to lose. Desperately, he tried to form his tunnel again. He started to picture his safe place but could not call it up out of his memory. *It's…the pain. I…can't think.* In his mind, the entity sent a reply.

Guess again. Garrett groaned and tried to remember…what? His mind went blank. He knew that he had a safe place, and he knew that both Melody and Molly were supposed to be there, but he could not form the picture in his mind. He felt amusement emanating from the entity.

"What…what have you done?" he gasped.

"I took it," said the baby. "Kiki dada doo." Garrett focused his attention on the infant, trying to fight through the pain. It stared at him with eyes that were now solid black. It was still grinning at him, only now that grin was both malicious and very much aware.

"Wh-what?"

"I took it, Daddy," said the baby in its high-pitched baby's voice. "I don't want you going anywhere without me. That would be bad, Daddy. That would be very, very bad. Aie! Babababababa!" The baby waved its arms and legs again.

"You…can't…"

"Oh yes, I can," giggled the baby. Despite its lack of teeth, its enunciation was perfect. "And I did. It's gone forever. And if you don't want me to take any more, you will behave yourself. Be a nice Daddy! Kay ba ba!" As suddenly as it had come, the pain evaporated. Garrett pitched forward onto the soggy sheet, gasping. "I can make the bad pain go away, Daddy," said the baby. "All you have to do is be good. Can you be good, Daddy? Can you?"

"What do you want?" gasped Garrett.

"Leave me and Mommy alone," said the baby. "She doesn't like you anymore. Just leave her alone and let us be together forever and ever."

"Why? Why her?"

"Because she's my mommy and I love her," said the baby. Garrett pushed himself up so that he could look at the thing pretending to be his daughter. He had lost his safe place, but he still remembered the beautiful young woman. He knew that his daughter was somewhere impossibly far away, but she was alive…perhaps more alive than she had ever been in this life. The baby grinned.

"No," whispered Garrett. "I won't let her go, you bastard. I won't let you have her." The pain crashed into him again. Incredibly, it was even worse than before. He did not even have the breath to scream.

"Bad Daddy," cried the baby. "Bad, bad Daddy!" The room started to grow dark, and Garrett understood that it was his vision that was fading. "Go away, Daddy," said the baby. "I'll come back tomorrow. You can change your mind then. Okay?" Garrett groaned, knowing that the entity meant what it said. It would come back tomorrow, and this scene would be repeated. Then if he did not agree, it would return again and again and again. He would never know rest or peace or…

"No!" he growled. He struggled up and forced his mind to focus. For just a moment, his eyesight cleared. He could feel the darkness closing in, but for a few precious seconds he was awake and aware. "No!" His right arm shot out, and he grabbed the baby by the neck.

Touching the thing's skin was like touching millions of stinging wasps. His palm burned with red fire, and he was certain that his skin was going to burn away. The baby hissed, and for just an instant Garrett saw two distinct emotions crawl across its dead face; surprise…and fear. He clenched his jaw and squeezed.

"Stop!" The baby gasped and wheezed. "Stop."

"No," Garrett growled. The pain soared to new heights. His mind screamed, and a red haze covered his sight. And still he squeezed. The baby's mouth opened impossibly wide as it tried to gulp in the air.

"Daaaaaadeeeeee," it hissed. "Pleeeeeaseeee stop hurrrrrtinnng meeeee."

"Give her back," growled Garrett. The darkness was closing in again. His mind had reached its limit and was shutting down. It could only endure so much. He focused every ounce of his dying will on the thing writhing in his grasp. "Give…her…back. Give…her…"

And the baby was gone. His hand was suddenly clenching the blood-soaked sheet. The pain vanished. His mind cleared, and his heart rate slowed to some semblance of normal. He felt his knee throbbing with the year-old pain that he had grown accustomed to and welcomed it. Compared with what he had just endured, it was a very small thing.

From the foot of the bed, he felt the entity. It was still there, watching him, but he could feel something else as well. The thing was weaker. Whatever power it had used to torture him had taken a toll. Garrett could also feel something else …uncertainty.

"Get out," he gasped. "You can't scare me anymore. I took your best shot, and you know it." From somewhere…else…he heard the reply.

I have barely begun to hurt you, sent the entity.

"I know you now," said Garrett, still gripping the sheet. "I know your name…John Gamble."

You know nothing.

"I know that I can take everything you have to give. And I know that I can take Melody away from you." He pointed at empty air. "I'm coming for you, John Gamble. Do you hear me? I'm coming for you, and I'm coming for Melody."

It will cost you everything. You only have so much to give. You have no idea how to use what is yours.

"I don't care."

Where is your safe place, Garrett Webb?

"It doesn't matter. Nothing matters, except my wife."

Stay.

"No."

Stay.

"No. I won't…" But the entity was gone. Garrett stared at the foot of the bed, still trying to process what had happened. The pain was gone, but it was still very much alive in his memory. He wondered dully if he could endure it a second time, even if it meant saving Melody. He fell back into the bed and winced. The sheets were damp with blood and sweat.

He nearly passed out trying to sit up, but he managed to get his feet on the floor. His night clothes were soaked, and his bare arms were streaked with blood. In addition, his head was throbbing, and his mouth was dry. He barely noticed. He had a feeling that from that moment on he would never have any difficulty enduring physical discomfort. Not after what the entity (John Gamble) had inflicted on him. He grabbed his cane and shuffled to the bathroom. On the way, he peeled off his nightclothes. He resolved to shower and spend the rest of the night in his recliner. He stepped into the bathroom, turned on the light, looked into the mirror, and groaned.

You only have so much to give, the entity had said. Garrett understood now. He had gone to bed as a twenty-seven-year-old man who, despite a bad knee, had been in moderately good shape. Now, staring back at him from the mirror, under a shock of pure white hair was the haggard face of a man of at least fifty.

Chapter 5

Confrontations

*I*t took him a week to recover. After the encounter, he lay unconscious in his chair for over forty-eight hours. Then he ate, slept, and ate some more.

The days were bad; the nights worse. The image of Melody in the grip of the entity haunted him. He would dream of her lying alone; tortured, abused…probably raped. He would wake up screaming her name. He had to find her. He had to save her, but his body refused to cooperate. The entity…he still could not think of it as a man who may or may not have carried the name of John Gamble…had left him physically devastated.

When he finally regained consciousness two days later, he could barely move. Every muscle in his body was on fire. It was several hours before he could even get out of his chair. He managed one trip to the kitchen…he was badly dehydrated again…and then slept for another twelve hours. When he awoke, it was still dark. He thumbed the light on his watch and saw that it was 5:38. He groaned in relief. There was no sign of the entity.

As it turned out, it did not return. Garrett could only hope that their second confrontation had weakened it as much as it had weakened him. He doubted it, but he had managed to get his licks in. Maybe that would be enough to keep it away long enough for him to recover.

At the end of a week, he was nearly back to his old strength, although his hair remained white and he still looked like a man who had seen the back side of fifty.

The wounds inflicted on his spirit were not so easily healed. Try as he might, he could not remember his safe place. He knew that he had one, or at least he used to have one, but he could no longer see it in his mind. The entity had stripped it away.

The darkness was still there as well, growing like a cancer. He did his best to ignore it. For the most part, he was successful, but it was slowly gaining strength with each passing day. He did not know how long he had before it overwhelmed him, and he had no idea what would happen to him when it did, but he did know that his time was short. Every minute that his weakness kept him in his chair was another minute that he was not looking for Melody.

You only have so much to give. He understood the entity's words all too well. Their fight had cost him maybe twenty years of his life. He had a sinking feeling that those years were gone forever.

That led him to a single devastating conclusion. The next time would more than likely kill him. Could he do that? Before his last encounter, he would have said yes without hesitation. Now, in the deepest place in his heart, he was ashamed to admit that he was not so sure. Even if he knew for certain that he could save Melody, he honestly did not know if he could endure that kind of agony again.

More than once, he toyed with the idea of obeying the entity. He could stay away. He would have to live with the grief and shame of abandoning his wife, but at least he would never have to endure that kind of pain again.

Each time he was tempted, he would shove the thought away, angry that he had even considered it, but it would always return. Each time, the urge to do nothing was just a little stronger. *She abandoned you. She walked away, arm in arm with that shrew of a mother. Let her save herself.* He tried to tell himself that the thoughts were not his own; that it was somehow the entity planting them into his mind in the same way it had planted the darkness into his heart. He did not believe it. The thoughts were his and his alone. In the end, he did the only thing he could. He stopped thinking about it and concentrated on healing.

The first thing he did as soon as he was able was quit his job. He did not dare go into the office. His appearance would spark too many questions. Donald Devers, his immediate supervisor, took it badly. Donald had a mean streak that kept the office in a state of constant tension. He refused to call anyone by their given names. Instead he made up nicknames that were just short of being cruel. Julie Scott was Scott On The Rocks, and Ross Daniels was, of course, Jack Daniels. He had christened Garrett 'Webhead'. During their brief phone conversation, Garrett took a perverse pleasure in listening to Donald go from angry to enraged in what had to be record time.

"You're going to quit without so much as a two-week notice?"

"I don't have a choice, Don. My wife…"

"I don't give a rat's ass about your wife, Webhead. You've got three projects pending, all of them with unbreakable deadlines. Do you have any idea what's going to happen to this company if we don't meet them?"

"To your job, you mean," said Garrett. "You couldn't care less about the company."

"That's enough. Get your ass back in here now, and I'll forget this conversation ever happened."

"Liar," said Garrett calmly. Now that he was committed, he felt quite free. "You'll get what you need out of me and then fire me."

"Shut up," snapped Donald. "Get in here now."

"No."

"Then you'd better understand this, buddy boy. I will personally call every firm in this area and tell them not to hire you. You won't work here again. I promise you that." Garrett could hear the panic peeking through the anger in Donald's voice. Not surprising, since his head would undoubtedly be on the chopping block when the deadlines came up short.

"I don't plan on working here again," said Garrett. "I'm leaving the state." In his mind's eye, he could see Donald pacing back and forth in his office.

"Look, Garrett," said Donald, reining in his temper. That made him smile. Donald never called him Garrett. He was getting desperate. "You can't run out on us like this. What about Julie? What about Ross? Are you going to leave them hanging? Do you know what this will do to them?"

"It will put a lot more on their plate," said Garrett. "But they'll handle it. They're good…better than you've ever given them credit for. The only job on the line will be yours."

"I won't let you quit," said Donald, raising his voice. His temper was getting the better of him. "I'll put it in your record that you were fired. You won't be able to get work anywhere in the country, much less this city."

"Whatever," said Garrett. "I've got better things to do. Goodbye." He broke the connection before Donald had a chance to reply. He stared at his cell phone. *I've just flushed my career down the toilet,* he thought. Then he decided that he honestly did not care.

He spent the rest of his convalescence playing detective. Molly's visit had provided him with a starting point. *Come back to me,* she said. That could only mean one thing. He had to go back to where she was buried.

It was not a pleasant thought. Neither he nor Melody had been able to bring themselves to hold any kind of funeral. They had purchased a simple plot in a secluded cemetery not far from their shattered house. Both of them had signed the proper papers, and both of them had been there when the tiny casket was lowered into the ground. It was the last time they had stood together as husband and wife.

So what do I do? Find Molly's grave and hold some kind of half-baked séance? That did not feel right, and he was learning to trust his feelings. He was certain that Molly's visitation had been real. He was also certain that his daughter was not in her grave. Oh, her tiny body might be resting there, but her soul, or spirit, or essence, or whatever it was called was somewhere else. Visiting her grave would be useless.

There was also the question of exactly where Melody might be. Was she still close by, maybe living with her mother? He did not think so. Why else would Molly send him to Florida? That meant that she had to be somewhere near Gainesville. Still, just how was he supposed to find her? Gainesville might be a small college city, but one person could hide there forever if they were so inclined.

Seven days after the attack, he stuffed a handful of clothes into a worn red, green and blue Tommy Hilfiger duffel bag. He still did not know just how far he could follow Melody's trail, but he had to at least make a start, and as much as he hated the idea, that trail began with Melinda Chance.

He shouldered the duffel, grabbed his cane and opened the door. He glanced back at his apartment. There was nothing, he realized, to indicate that the unique individual known as Garrett Webb had lived there. The apartment was sterile, and as he gave it one last look, he realized that he really had never lived in it. He had merely existed in it for a short time. He shook his head, closed the door and walked away.

On the way to the Chance home, he stopped by the bank and withdrew a thousand dollars in cash. He debated closing his accounts but then decided that it would not be a good idea to lug so much cash around.

He had his VISA checking card, as well as an American Express. That would be more than enough to get him to Florida and sustain him for quite a while.

Twenty minutes later, he arrived at the Chance home. It was in an older middle class neighborhood, the kind where every house pretty much looked the same as its neighbors. He stared at the house, a single story red brick model. It was small but tidy. Melody's husband had left long ago, just after Darrin was born. Melinda had worked two and sometimes three jobs to keep her family afloat. She had poured her life into her children, determined that they would have better lives than the one fate had dealt her.

She succeeded. Both Darrin and Arvin made it through college and were moderately successful in the business world. She was tough, determined and resourceful. She was also mean and bigoted, not just against white men, but against men in general. No man would ever be good enough for her baby girl.

Neither of her sons lived at home, but both of them owned houses close by, and Darrin worked in an office less than five minutes away. A single phone call, and he would come running.

Garrett sat in his car for almost an hour before he got up the nerve to get out and ring the doorbell. He heard it buzz and waited. His knee was throbbing, and he tried to put as much weight on his cane as he could. After several seconds and no response, he rang again. He could almost feel Melinda peering out through the peephole. He was just about to ring a third time when the door flew open. Melinda Chance stood there with fire in her eyes and a wicked looking baseball bat in her hands.

"How dare you," she began, but then she took a good look at him. Her eyes grew wide with shock. "What happened to…?" Garrett was ready.

"John Gamble," he said, wondering if the name could possibly have any meaning for her. It did. Melinda flinched as if she had been slapped. Her free hand came up as if to ward off a blow. Her mouth opened, closed and opened again. The bat wavered and then lowered. Garrett's shot had not only hit its target, it had driven deep.

"What do you know…?" Her voice was a harsh rasp.

"I know that he did this to me," said Garrett, not giving her a chance to finish. "I know that Melody's in trouble, and I know that John Gamble is that trouble." Melinda stared at him some more.

"How could you know that name?" she demanded. From the moment Garrett had decided to see her, he had been wondering what he would say if she asked him that question. Now, seeing her reaction to the name, he decided on the simple truth.

"I've met him," he said. Melinda's eyes grew wide.

"You lie," she snapped.

"You know better," said Garrett. "I can see it in your eyes."

"You need to leave."

"Where's Melody?"

"Get out. Get out before…"

"Before what? You call the police? One of your useless sons comes running? I'm sure you've already called Darrin. He's probably on his way here now, but I couldn't care less. Where's Melody, Melinda?" He could see the hatred and loathing in her eyes, but he could also see the fear. She was terrified. He reined in his anger. "Her spirit came to me," he said, lowering his voice. "It wasn't a dream, Melinda. It was real. She came to me, and she begged me to save her."

"That's…that's impossible. She wouldn't…she couldn't…"

"He came as well…John Gamble, or something Melody called John Gamble. He did this to me, and he took Melody's spirit away. He's got her somewhere, and I think you know where. Tell me, Melinda. For her sake, tell me." His former mother-in-law took a step backward. For a moment, Garrett was sure that she was going to use her bat. Then he saw the unthinkable. He saw a single tear roll down Melinda's cheek. She did not have to say anything. He understood.

"You don't know," he said. She shook her head.

"She left almost four weeks ago," she said. "She wouldn't tell any of us where she was going." For a moment, her face grew hard and her hatred resurfaced. "We thought that she might be going back to you. My boys took turns watching your place, but she never showed." Garrett could only shake his head.

"Who is John Gamble?" he asked. "*What* is he, and what does he have to do with Melody?"

"That's not your business," snapped Melinda. "It's family, and you aren't family."

"Tell it to Melody," replied Garrett. "She came to *me*." Melinda looked away, but Garrett could still see her shame. His insight flared.

"She came to you too," he said flatly. "She begged you to help her." Melinda flinched again, and again Garrett saw the truth. "You can't," he said. "Whatever has her has some kind of hold on you too."

"What do you know?" she hissed, whirling back to face him. "What do you know about anything?"

"I know that Melody needs my help," said Garrett. "I know that whoever or whatever John Gamble is, he stole a big chunk of my life." He met Melinda's eyes and suddenly realized that he had just made his decision. "And I know that I'm going to get her back. I don't care what it costs me, Melinda. I'm going to save her." Melinda looked away again. Garrett pressed his advantage.

"Who is John Gamble? I know how much you hate me, but you must know that I'm going to do everything I can to save her. Who is he, Melinda?" Melinda gripped the bat until her fingers went white. Garrett could see that her hatred of him was going toe-to-toe with her fear for her daughter. He waited, but before she could answer, a black Volvo came screeching to a halt behind him. He turned, knowing exactly what he would see. Sure enough, Darrin Chance was climbing out of his car. His eyes were blazing, and his mouth was etched into a feral snarl. He slammed his door shut and stormed toward him.

"I warned you," he shouted, pointing at Garrett. "Now I'm going to take you apart. Mom, go inside."

"Stay where you are, boy!" Darrin jerked to a stop.

"Get inside, Mom," he said again.

"You stay right there," ordered Melinda. "I mean it now. Don't you come any closer."

"Mom…"

"Hush," snapped Melinda. She turned her attention back to Garrett.

"You save my baby," she said in a low, dangerous voice. "You give me your word."

"I'll save her," said Garrett. "Not for you, and not for me, but for her. I love her. I always have, and I always will."

"LIAR!" This was from Darrin.

"Shut up, boy," snapped Melinda. She turned back to Garrett.

"You'll have to go back to Florida," she said, "back to where you were." Garrett nodded. He knew as much.

"Why? What's down there?"

"Our past," whispered Melinda. Garrett could see that she was struggling with the words. It was as if something was fighting her. "And our future. I thought that when she came back, she might…but now…"

"I don't understand."

"You will," said Melinda. "When you get there, look for…Gamble's Run." Sweat was starting to bead on her forehead.

"'Gamble's Run'? As in John Gamble?" Melinda nodded, and then winced. She rubbed her chest. "Are you all right?"

"Gamble's Run. Do you understand? Find…Gamble's Run." She backed away, gasping for breath. "That's…all I can tell you. Now get out of here, and don't you ever come back." Garrett opened his mouth, but Melinda had already shut the door. He stared after her for long seconds. Then he turned to leave. Darrin was still there, and he was still angry. Garrett eased down the porch steps, hoping that the oldest Chance son would have the good sense to leave him alone. Of course, he did not. As Garrett made to pass him, he grabbed his arm.

"My turn," he growled. His other hand curled into a fist, and he pulled it back, ready to strike.

What happened next would haunt Garrett for the rest of his life. The instant Darrin touched him, he felt the darkness seethe. It boiled up, triggering a kind of anger that he had never known. Then a small part of it flew out of him. He could almost see it as lanced away and flew straight into Darrin. Part of him was horrified, but another part was grimly satisfied. He felt his mouth curl into a sneer.

"Don't you ever touch me again," he rasped. Darrin probably did not even hear him. He released his grip on Garrett's arm and stumbled away, his hands clawing at his chest.

"What did you do to me?" he screamed. "Dear God, what did you do?" At that instant, the door flew open. Melinda stood there, only now instead of a bat, she was holding a shotgun. She pointed it straight at him.

"You leave him be," she shouted. "Get out now, or I will kill you. I swear it on my daughter's life, Garrett Webb. I will kill you!" Garrett did not have to be told twice. He got into his car and drove off. He glanced in the rear-view mirror as he drove away and saw Melinda coming down to help her son. Then he turned a corner, and they were gone.

"Gamble's Run," he whispered. It was a start, but that knowledge had been bought with a price. He now knew a terrible truth about the darkness. He could force it into others, just as the entity had forced it into him. Far worse was the fact that it was now weaker inside of him. He could only wonder if he could get rid of all of it by doing the same thing to others. The idea made him sick to his stomach.

"You bastard," he whispered, rubbing his eyes. "You knew this would happen, didn't you?" The entity did not answer, and Garrett was fairly certain that it did not hear him. Maybe it was still nursing its wounds.

There was nothing left for him to do. He had severed every tie. The only thing that mattered now was finding

Melody. He made his way to the interstate and set his course due south.

Chapter 6

Dead Neighborhood

Three days later, he stood silent before a vacant lot. The ground was barren, the only exception being a single scraggly dandelion that had somehow managed to take root in the far corner. Its wilted leaves lay flat on the ground, and its stalk was bent double, as if bowing in unconditional surrender. Life it seemed, even in the form of the heartiest of weeds, was forbidden to flourish in this place.

The sink hole was gone, filled in with tons of dirt. A waist-high chain link fence guarded the parameter. A bright yellow sign, bolted to a small gate, warned anyone who might want to do a little unofficial exploring that this place was forbidden. Nothing beyond the fence hinted at the tragic events of over a year ago.

The destruction that night had been catastrophic. The grim tally; four houses swallowed whole and fifteen people, including one beautiful little girl, dead. The rescue workers managed to pull twelve others out of the wreckage. The entire neighborhood had been condemned and evacuated. The surviving families would be battling with their respective insurance companies for years.

The tragedy had made national news. FOX, CNN and MSNBC had spent days replaying video from that night. Experts had tried to explain how so many sinkholes could open so quickly, but in the end it had baffled everyone. The odds of such an event happening even once were beyond astronomic. A team of geologists from the University of Florida had set up shop in one of the empty houses. They were conducting an intensive study of the entire area, trying to figure out just how such a disaster could happen and maybe prevent it from happening again.

It was early, just a few minutes past nine, but the Florida heat and humidity were already in full swing. Silence, heavy and unnatural, hung over the deserted neighborhood. During their brief stay, both Garrett and Melody had constantly argued with the trio of students that rented the house across the street. They were coming and going at all hours of the night, and their cars were constantly blasting whatever heavy metal song that happened to be called up on their iPods.

A handful of children used to live nearby, some with one parent, some with both. They were a constant but pleasant nuisance, riding their bicycles up and down the street, playing tag or hide-n-seek, or just running and screaming for no apparent reason. It added up to a very active, very loud neighborhood.

Now the houses stood vacant. The cracked driveways were empty, as were the backyard playgrounds. Mailboxes hung open, empty mouths hungry for letters that would never arrive. There was no music playing or engines revving. In a single night, this neighborhood had died in agony.

The silence was oppressive. It shrouded each and every house, as if preparing them for burial. Even the geology team was nowhere to be seen. Garrett stared at the lot, trying to sort through the cascade of feelings and memories that threatened to overwhelm him. He could see a grinning Molly running naked across the small front yard, chased by an exasperated Melody. He could see himself turning into the driveway, his two favorite girls waiting at the front door, ready to welcome him home. He could see…

"Excuse me, sir." Startled out of his memories, Garrett jumped. The voice came from behind him. He turned and came face to face with a pretty young woman of about twenty. She was short, barely topping five feet, and her straight brown hair fell to her shoulders. She was wearing jeans and a blue denim work shirt. She held a clipboard in her right hand and a pen in her left. On her right ear was a blue tooth attachment for a cell phone. A tiny blue light on its side blinked at regular intervals. Garrett realized that she was undoubtedly a member of the geology team from the university. Realizing that she had startled him, she took a step back.

"Sorry," she said, smiling. "I didn't mean to frighten you." Garrett managed a weak smile.

"No problem," he said. "I guess I was lost in my thoughts."

"It's just that you're not supposed to be here," said the young woman. "This entire neighborhood is off limits."

"I know," said Garrett. "I just needed to see it again." The woman's eyes widened.

"You were here, weren't you?" she said. "The night it happened, I mean." Garrett nodded.

"That used to be my home," he said, pointing at the lot. The young woman bit her lip and looked down at her clipboard. After she leafed through a few pages, she looked back up at him.

"Are you Mr. Webb?" Again, Garrett nodded. The woman frowned and checked her information again.

"There must be some mistake," she said. "I have here that Garrett Webb was twenty-seven years old." She looked at him, her eyes asking the question. Garrett shrugged.

"You're dead on," he said. "I'm Garrett Webb, I'm twenty-seven…twenty-eight now…and I really did live here. If it helps, I'm younger than I look. That night took a lot out of me." He looked down, hoping that the lie was convincing enough. The woman's face mirrored her doubts, but she nodded sympathetically.

"I'm sorry," she said. Then she held out her right hand. "I'm Jean," she said. "Jean Francis." Garrett took her hand automatically, shook it once and let it go. Jean glanced over at the lot. "It must have been terrible," she said.

"Yes, it was," replied Garrett. Jean consulted her clipboard again. Garrett heard her draw a sharp breath.

"Your daughter was Marlene Webb?" He had been expecting the question, but it still hit him like a runaway truck. To hear his daughter's name coming from the lips of a stranger was almost more than he could bear.

"Yeah," he whispered, "but we called her Molly." Jean saw his pain and looked away.

"I'm sorry," she said again. "I didn't mean to sound so calloused about it." She managed an uncomfortable smile. "I can't imagine what you must be feeling right now."

"Forget it," said Garrett. "I just needed to see this place again. I thought…"

"What?" asked Jean.

"Nothing," said Garrett, giving the lot one last glance. "There's nothing here for me. I probably shouldn't have come. I'm sorry to have troubled you." He brushed past Jean and limped toward his car.

"No trouble," she said. "I hope your wife is all right." Something in the way she said 'wife' brought Garrett up short. He turned back to her.

"Do you know Melody?" he asked. Jean shook her head.

"I only met her once, a few weeks ago when she stopped by. Some of the other residents have come here; not many, but a few. I guess they're like you. They just need to see the place again."

"When?" demanded Garrett, taking a step toward the young woman. "When was she here?" Jean's eyes widened, and she backed away. Realizing that he had just frightened her, Garrett held up both hands, palms out. "I'm sorry," he said. "I don't mean any harm. I just need to find Melody. You said she was here?" Jean nodded uncertainly.

"Two weeks ago," she said. "My team and I were doing soundings." Garrett shook his head. "We set off small seismic charges and record the results with ultrasound. It lets us see deep into the earth." Garrett nodded.

"She came here, to look at the lot?" he asked.

"We let her stay for a bit," she said. "We couldn't bear to send her away. I stayed with her." She eyed

Garrett. "I'm sorry. I just thought that you would have…"

"We've been separated for over a year," he said flatly, then shrugged. "For that matter, we've been separated since that night. Did she seem all right to you?" Jean hesitated. "I promise that I'm not trying to cause her any more grief," he said. "She disappeared and didn't tell anyone where she was going. If I can just let her family know that she's all right, I'll leave her alone." That was a blatant lie, but he thought he sounded sincere enough. Jean seemed to buy it, at any rate. She cocked her head, giving Garrett an appraising look.

"No," she said after a moment, "she really didn't seem all that well." Garrett nodded.

"How so?" he asked.

"Well, for starters, she looked exhausted," said Jean. "More than exhausted, in fact; like she was about to keel over. And she was nervous. She kept looking around. It was almost as if she thought she was being watched."

"Anything else?" asked Garrett. Jean thought some more.

"She…" She shook her head.

"Please," said Garrett softly. "I need to know."

"She looked scared," said Jean after a moment. "In fact, she looked downright terrified." Her eyes narrowed. "She wouldn't have been afraid of you, now would she?" It took Garrett a moment to realize what she was implying.

"No! Oh God, no," he said, taking a step back. "I swear to you, I would never hurt her. I…"

"You still love her," finished Jean. "Yeah, I get it." She eyed him carefully and then decided to give him the benefit of the doubt. "Okay," she said. "I guess I believe you."

"Thanks," said Garrett. He heard the sarcasm in his voice and tried to smile. Judging from the way Jean was eyeing him again, he did not quite pull it off. "I'm really sorry," he said. "It's been a bad year." Jean nodded, softening. "Did Mel say anything at all about where she might be heading?"

"No," said Jean. "In fact, she hardly spoke at all. She just said she wanted to visit the place where her daughter died. I tried to talk to her, but…no, she didn't say anything about where she was going." Garrett nodded. It was a long shot, but he was still disappointed.

"Jean! Hey, Jean!" The shout came from behind them. Both Garrett and Jean turned in time to see a tall, well-built man in his mid-thirties emerge from behind one of the nearby houses. If everything about Jean said 'student', then everything about the newcomer screamed 'professor'. He was wearing khaki work pants and a matching shirt. On his head was a blue cap featuring an orange 'F' and an angry alligator on the front…the mascot of the University of Florida.

Jean waved him over. Garrett could not help but notice how her body language changed as he drew closer. It was subtle but obvious. *Looks like the professor and Mary Ann here have been doing a little more than digging,* he thought. Then he blushed and looked away. It was none of his business.

"Hey, Bob," Jean called as the man drew near. "This is Garrett Webb. He used to live in the house on that lot. Mr. Webb, this is my boss, Professor Robert Davies." Davies held out a calloused hand, and Garrett took it.

"Good to meet you," said Davies.

"You remember his wife," said Jean. "She came by a few weeks ago." Davies nodded.

"Of course," he said. "I'm very sorry for what happened to you." Garrett nodded his thanks, although he could see that Davies was just being polite. The professor turned his attention to Jean.

"Linda needs you," he said. "They're ready to set off another charge." Jean nodded.

"It was good to meet you," she said to Garrett. "I hope your wife's okay." With a wave and a nod, she trotted off, disappearing around the corner of the nearest house.

"I'm afraid that I'm going to have to ask you to leave," said Davies. "This entire area still isn't stable. The last time we set off a charge, we caused another sinkhole; a small one, and it didn't do any damage, but the way this place is, you never know."

"Has anything like this ever happened before?" asked Garrett. Davies shook his head.

"Never," he said. "We still don't know what caused it."

"The drought…"

"That was only a part of it," said Davies, interrupting. "The water table was low, but it's been lower. This should never have happened."

"I didn't live in Florida long," said Garrett. "What's the water table?"

"The underground water level," said Davies. Garrett noted the way the professor leaned forward as he spoke. He seemed to have forgotten that moments ago he had ordered Garrett off the property. Here was a man who was deeply in love with his work. "The entire state is honeycombed with underground rivers," he continued. "We've had cave divers go down in one spring and come up miles away." Garrett shuddered. He had seen documentaries on cave diving. The idea of crawling through narrow underwater passages made for good nightmares. Davies noticed his discomfort and smiled. This time it was genuine.

"You wouldn't catch me doing it either," he said, "although we had a lot of fun following them. They wore transponders that we could track on the surface. We followed their trail through back yards, gas stations and even a Sonny's Barbeque. I think we made a few people uncomfortable. They didn't like the idea that someone was swimming a hundred feet beneath their feet."

"I can understand that," muttered Garrett. He looked down at the ground, half-expecting one of the divers to come bursting through the dirt. Davies nodded and waved an arm at the neighborhood.

"We think we walk on solid ground," he said, "but underneath there's a lot of empty space...well, empty space and water." He glanced at his watch. "Listen," he said, "I hate to do this to you, but you really do need to leave. If the board finds out that I let someone in here while we were doing soundings, they'll have my head, not to mention my funding."

"No problem," said Garrett. "I saw what I came to see." He offered his hand, and Davies took it. Then the two men started off in opposite directions, but suddenly Garrett stopped. It was a shot in the dark, he knew, but at the moment, it was the only shot he had.

"Hey Professor," he called to the retreating Davies. Davies stopped and turned. Both his irritation and impatience were evident.

"Mr. Webb..." he began.

"Just a quick question," said Garrett, limping over to him. "Please." Davies frowned but nodded.

"Have you ever heard of anything called Gamble's Run?" Davies frowned.

"Gamble's Run? No, I don't think so. Is it a street or something?" Garrett shrugged.

"I have no idea," he said. "Melody mentioned it to her mother, but neither of us has any idea what she was talking about."

"Sorry," said Davies. "But I've never heard of it."

"How about John Gamble?" asked Garrett. "Does that name mean anything to you?" Davies' eyes widened.

"Of course," he said. "John Gamble is something of a local legend. He was responsible for the Slave Canal." He pursed his lips. "That could be what you mean. I don't think I've ever heard it called 'Gamble's Run' before, but the name fits." Garrett felt his heart do a double thump. Had he actually struck pay dirt?

"The Slave Canal?" he asked.

"It was dug in the 1800s," said Davies, "Just before the Civil War. Like Gamble, it's a bit of a legend around here, except that it still exists."

"What's…"

"I'm really sorry, Mr. Webb," said Davies impatiently, "but my team is waiting for me. I have to get to work, and you really need to leave." He started off but then relented. "You can probably Google it if you want," he called over his shoulder. "It's not well known, but the locals love it, and I hear that it's a great place to canoe."

"Thanks," called Garrett. "I really appreciate it. You've been an incredible help." His sincerity softened Davies' attitude. The professor smiled and waved a farewell. Then he trotted away. Garrett watched him, envying the casual way he ran.

"Forget it," he huffed and headed back to his car. His running days were gone forever. Melody was gone too, but maybe not forever. There was still a chance he could get her back. For the first time, he had a lead. "Just hang on, Mel," he muttered as he slid behind the wheel. "Whatever it takes, just hang on." He drove out of the neighborhood, knowing in his heart that he would never return. "The Slave Canal," he said aloud. As soon as he got back to his motel room, he would take Davies' suggestion and 'Google' it. Then, if he needed to know more, he would head to the university.

His heart raged at the delay. Somewhere, if she was still alive, his wife was being brutalized by something so vile that his mind could not comprehend it. She could be dying. She could be dead. He had to find her, but he needed to know where to look. Like it or not, he was going to have to do some serious research.

"The Slave Canal," he said again as he turned onto the main highway. "What the heck is the Slave Canal, and what the heck do it and John Gamble mean to Melody?" He did not have the answer, but at least he had a starting point. His next stop would be the university. "I've got work to do," he whispered. "The question is, do I have time to do it?"

Chapter 7

Visions and Patterns

Surfing the Internet provided Garrett with plenty of information but little insight. After he left Davies and company, he found the nearest Starbucks, set up shop in a booth in the back and got to work. Two hours later, he closed his laptop and finished off his third latté. His eyes were glazed and his head was buzzing, courtesy of the heavy doses of caffeine.

Davies had been right. The information was sparse, but it was there to anyone who bothered to look for it. The Slave Canal was one of those well kept secrets known to the local residents, geologists from the university and a handful of out-of-town nature lovers.

The naturalists loved it because it was a stunning place to travel via canoe. The locals loved it because of its historical significance. The geologists loved it because the remains of a far older civilization they named the Paleo could be found there. Artifacts thousands of years old had been unearthed. Expeditions were mounted every year, and it seemed that every year they came away with a new discovery. Some of the geologists had nicknamed the canal 'Florida's Lost Atlantis'.

Garrett was able to dig up enough information so that he now understood how and why the canal was created. There was, unfortunately, absolutely nothing on the various websites that provided any clue as to the relationship between it and Melody. He sat back and rubbed his tired eyes.

The facts were straightforward. John Gamble had been a wealthy cotton grower living in central Florida in the 1800s. He was a part of a loose consortium of landowners and businessmen who needed a faster way to get their cotton to the Gulf of Mexico. Poor roads made transportation difficult and often impossible. The Wacissia, the nearest river, had a bad habit of disappearing underground for several miles at a stretch. It ended in a mazelike swamp that the locals called, charmingly enough, The Warriors.

Gamble commissioned the canal in 1831. The plan was to link the Wacissia with the Aucilla River, which flowed unobstructed to the Gulf. The canal would be about two and a half miles long and deep enough to allow the barges to pass. They could then make the run to the gulf in record time.

It was a devastating failure. The canal had to be dug by hand, and that meant that it had to be dug by slaves. The idea made Garrett shudder. The temperature that day had spiked at ninety-five, and the humidity had made being outdoors nearly unbearable. What must those poor men have endured while digging the canal? How many of them died in the process, laboring in the disease infested swamps?

From the beginning, the canal did not work. It had been dug too shallow. During the dry season, the water level sank so low that it was next to impossible to get the barges through. They kept getting hung up on the canal bed, not to mention the constantly falling branches from the trees that lined both banks.

Then, not long after the canal was finished, the railroad appeared and took over the transportation duties. A few decades later, the Civil War broke out, and that took care of the slaves. The canal was abandoned, left to stand as a silent indictment of John Gamble's folly.

Garrett found a portrait of the man himself on the website of a local newspaper. He seemed unremarkable in every way. Soft, almost effeminate features accompanied by a gentle smile gave him a friendly, caring look. His nose had just a hint of a hook, and his brown hair was cropped short. In the portrait, he wore a white scarf and a dark, high collared coat. He seemed in every way to be a typical country gentleman of the 1800s. Garrett could easily picture him hosting a gala at his mansion, inviting the local belles to attend in their finest apparel. There was no hint of a man who casually sent hundreds of slaves into a hellish environment just to get his cotton to market a little faster. Garrett had stared at the picture.

Is it you? Are you the monster who stole twenty years of my life? It did not feel right. He could not match the man on his screen with the creature that had invaded his apartment.

He could find no mention of Gamble's Run. None of the websites used that name, although it certainly seemed to fit. There had been an effort some time back by a few low level bureaucrats at the state capital to change the name from the Slave Canal to the Cotton Run Canal. The term Slave Canal was deemed racist and labeled as hate speech. The idea had been vehemently opposed by the local residents, both black and white. They considered the Slave Canal an important part of their heritage, something that should be remembered for what it was and what it represented. The proposal quickly died.

Garrett's next step was the local Kinkos, where he printed out every scrap of relevant material off the 'Web, including a map of the entire area. It all added up to a stack of over thirty pages. By the time he got back to his motel, it was dark. He spread the pages out over the bed and got to work.

The canal joined the Wacissia and the Aucilla rivers close to Nutall Rise. As far as he could tell, Nutall Rise was a tiny hill, a pimple on the mostly flat Florida countryside. Day trippers used it as an embarkation point where they launched their canoes.

Frustration was setting in. He had learned a great deal, but was no closer to finding Melody. He tossed the printouts on the floor and flopped back into the lumpy motel bed. The sheets smelled of dust and age. He stared at the ceiling, trying to make sense of the mound of information he had ingested. The caffeine was washing out of his system. His thoughts were becoming muddy, and he could feel the beginnings of a first class headache coming on.

"What am I missing?" he said aloud. "The Slave Canal, Gamble's Run, John Gamble, and Melody. What's the connection?" There was none that he could see. Melody had never spoken of her family line. It was possible that she was a descendant of one of the slaves who dug the canal, but if so, then why was the Gamble entity targeting her? There must be hundreds, perhaps thousands of descendants of those slaves. Were they all being tormented?

"What am I missing?" he asked again, closing his eyes. The events of the day, coupled with his long trip, caught up to him. His mind grew fuzzy, and he fell into a deep sleep.

#

The demolished house slid into the gaping maw that was the sinkhole. The wood shattered with a series of loud pops as the entire structure was sucked into the earth. Garrett and Melody watched in horror as the most precious thing in their lives was swallowed as well. Garrett screamed and tried to crawl toward the hole, but one of the rescue workers held him back.

"Let me go," he cried. "Please, you've got to let me save Molly."

"Too late," said the worker. "She's gone."

"No! I can still save her." He tried again. "Get…off…me!" He kicked and punched but could not break free. Bruised and bloody, Melody began crawling toward the hole.

"Melody", he cried out. "Wait! You can't…I can't lose you too!" He lunged forward, but again the worker pulled him back. "Please," he whimpered. "Save her. Save my wife."

"I can't," said the worker. "The hole's got her now."

"NO!" Garrett lunged forward again, and this time he managed to get loose. He fell to the ground and scrambled toward Melody, who had now reached the edge of the sinkhole.

"It'll get you too," shouted the worker, but Garrett ignored him. He clawed his way forward. "Wait for me, Mel," he shouted. "Just…wait!"

Light exploded all around him. He slammed his eyes shut. So intense was the light that for a terrifying moment he was certain that he had been blinded. He buried his head in his arms, his nose pressed against the dry ground. Angry purple flashes exploded against his eyelids, but after a moment they subsided. He managed to open his eyes. He looked in the direction of the sinkhole and screamed.

The light shot into the night sky, emanating from deep within the earth. It was green; mean, disease-ridden green. Garrett squeezed his eyes shut again. He knew that if he looked at the light too long, it would stab into his eyes, invade his body, and eat him alive.

Then a wonderful thing happened. Garrett's conscious mind decided that enough was enough. A different kind of light flared. It did not begin to match the intensity of the vile green glow that vomited out of the sinkhole, nor could it compete with the darkness that was eating away at his soul, but in its own way, it was powerful. It surrounded him, seeping over him like a second skin. He felt it bathe him in its warm embrace. Then it hardened, and Garrett realized that it was now a shield…a shield strong enough to repel the sinkhole light because…

Because I'm dreaming, he thought. Then he paused, uncertain. Everything felt far too real. He could hear the screams of those being pulled from the sinkholes by the rescue workers. He could feel the ground beneath him and smell its arid dryness. *Am I dreaming?* he wondered. It was a reasonable question. He had experienced lucid dreaming only once in his life. Then, he had devised a simple test. *If I'm dreaming, then I can fly,* he thought. *I'll open my eyes, and I'll be floating above the ground.*

He opened his eyes.

He was floating an inch above the bare earth, his arms stretched out to either side. *Yes!* He grabbed on to his courage and again looked at the sinkhole. Now, with his shield…his reality shield…he was able to gaze straight into the heart of the light. A dark silhouette lay on the ground, inching toward the edge of the hole. *Not this time.*

It's too late, said a still, small voice. It was not the voice of the rescuers. Nor was it Molly's voice, the entity, or even Melody. It was his voice. *Melody's not there, and Molly's dead. You know this. There's nothing you can do.* His vision wavered. The shield grew brighter, and suddenly he was glowing like a miniature sun. He could feel his mind expanding. He was waking up. *None of that,* he growled. He was not quite sure how he did it, but he managed to reign in his shield. His vision stabilized. He was still asleep, and still in command of his dream.

Pulling his arms back, he shot forward, flying just inches above the ground. When he got to the edge of the sinkhole, Melody was already tottering. In seconds, she would be over the edge. *Not this time,* he thought again. *Molly's dead. Maybe Melody is as well, but right here, right now, I can still save them.* He reached the edge and flinched. The sheer force coming from the malignant green light forced him back. He snarled at it and again pushed forward.

I've seen it before, but where? It was a fleeting thought, and it vanished immediately. The light fought him, but his shield held and he managed to reach Melody. She was lying face down on the ground, her head and shoulders hanging over the edge of the hole.

He grabbed her outstretched arm and rolled her over. Her eyes were closed, and she seemed to be sleeping.

Mel! Wake up! he shouted or tried to shout. His voice was thin and empty. He tried again but could barely manage a whisper. He shook her hard, but she did not respond. *Let her go, you bastard,* he growled. He planted his feet on the ground, got his arms under her and scooped her up. She weighed nothing at all. Then he turned and faced the green light. *My dream,* he thought. *My rules.*

Cradling Mel in his arms like Superman might cradle Lois Lane, he shot into the night sky. *Up, up and away,* he thought, giggling. The light faded, and he felt its power fade with it. *It has a range,* he thought. *Somehow, it's tied to the earth. It can't reach me up here.*

He stopped his ascent, hovering in the black velvet sky. There were stars everywhere. They blazed with a brilliance and glory that he had never seen and could never have imagined. Their light was like a soothing balm. He felt it wash over him, bringing peace and healing. He reveled in it. *You may be strong,* he thought, looking down at the now dim green glow, *but you're not all powerful. There are greater things than you…things that you will never be able to touch or defile.* The knowledge comforted and strengthened him.

Given a choice, he might have remained there forever, but he was not yet done with his work. Dream or not, he still had one more person to save. Gathering his courage, he held Melody close, feeling her warm skin against his. Then he dove straight into the light.

The instant he penetrated it, he knew that it was aware. He could feel its rage at the intrusion, and it put forth all its considerable might to repel him. His shield shrank, but it continued to hold. He plunged down into the sinkhole. The lip of the hole flashed past, and then he was flying deep underground. *I'm taking them both,* he said to something that might or might not be listening.

His shattered house came into view. Now it was split into four equal parts. He could easily see what remained of Molly's bedroom. There was her crib, still intact. He swooped down to it but found it empty. *Molly! Where are you, baby? Daddy's here. Daddy's come to save you!*

I'm not here, Dad. The voice came from behind him. Still floating, he turned and saw his daughter, not as an infant, but as the full grown woman he had met in his safe place. She was looking at him with what could only be described as exasperated love.

Molly! His voice was still impossibly thin. *Come on, baby. Let's get out of here.* Molly shook her head.

You're going the wrong way, Dad. You've got to go up again. You need to see the big picture.

Molly?

Dad, listen to me. Get back into the sky. You've got to go up now. You need to see the pattern. She pointed to the sky. *Go, Dad! Go now!*

But...

Dad! Go! So strong was the command that he obeyed immediately. Clutching Melody, he shot up through the shaft of light. The edge of the hole flashed by, but he ignored it. Maybe it was his own mind calling out to him, or maybe it really was Molly somehow communicating through his dream. It did not matter. Something was demanding his attention, and he knew with the certainty that only comes in dreams that whatever it was, it was vitally important.

The light faded as he gained altitude until it disappeared entirely. He was back in the sky, floating among the brilliant stars. He slowed, stopped and looked down. *Dear God.* He was floating high above the Earth, so high that he could easily its curve.

The Florida peninsula sprawled out below him. He could see several cities shining in the night, complimented by dozens of lesser glows that also indicated a human presence. There was the Gulf of Mexico and the Atlantic Ocean, both shimmering under a brilliant moon. *Moon?* He glanced up and saw that there was now a full moon. He looked down again, wondering just what he was supposed to see. *What the…?*

The cities were gone, extinguished, as were the smaller towns. He squinted, trying to make out any kind of detail, but he could see nothing. The more he stared, the more uncomfortable he became. He could trace the outline of the state but nothing more. He suddenly felt as if he was staring at a Florida-shaped black hole.

There was a flash of light. It was faint, but it was there. He glanced in its direction, but it disappeared, leaving nothing but the inky blackness. *Imagination?* He shook his head. *No way. Not here, and not now.* He looked over at the gulf, letting his mind wonder. The light flashed, but when he looked again, it was gone. *Got it.*

He relaxed his eyes, letting them slide out of focus. The instant he did, the light returned. This time, he did not look directly at it. He kept staring at the gulf, watching with his peripheral vision. It was a pinpoint, but it was there. It flared, followed almost immediately by another, and another, and another. They spread out across the state, winking like tiny Christmas lights, although there was nothing festive about them. They all glowed with the same sick green light that filled the sinkhole.

You need to see the pattern. Molly's voice echoed in his mind, guiding him. The dots continued to flash, and he realized what he was seeing. Each and every dot was a sinkhole, and each was infected with the same diseased light. *The big picture.* He understood now. There was a pattern. There was…

Melody stirred in his arms. He looked down at her and saw that she was regaining consciousness.

"Easy, baby," he whispered. "I've got you." Melody moaned. Suddenly, she began to struggle. Surprised, Garrett tightened his grip. "Melody, I've got you. You're safe." She moaned again. Her arms flailed. One of them caught Garrett's temple in a glancing blow. Dream or not, the blow staggered him, and he nearly lost his grip. "Melody! Calm down!" He tried to pull her close, but she pushed away. Then her eyes opened. Light blazed out of them, the same light that infested the sinkhole.

"Let…me…go!" Garrett gasped. He knew that voice. It did not belong to Melody. It belonged to the entity that had taken her. The circuits in his mind connected, and his memory flashed.

That's where I've seen it before, he thought, meaning the green light. Even in his dream state, he suddenly felt sick. He remembered the night of the sinkhole. He remembered trying to console Melody, and he remembered how, for just a moment, her eyes had flashed green. *Even then,* he thought. *He had a hold on her even then.* There was a blur of motion. He did not even see Melody's fist until it had already collided with his cheek. Stunned, he fell backward. Melody shoved against him, and this time he was unable to hold on.

"NO!" It was too late. Melody floated free. She snarled at him. Then something big, powerful, and invisible grabbed her. Garrett felt rather than saw a great hand, connected to an impossibly long arm, reach up out of the sinkhole and drag her down. She disappeared into the gaping hole far below. "NO!" he screamed again. He aimed himself straight at the sinkhole, but before he could move, he felt another presence.

Dad! Stop!

Not now, Molly! He's got her.

Yes, he does, said Molly. *And you're not going to get her back his way. The time will come when you will fight for her, but now is not that time.*

Shut up, snarled Garrett. *I've had enough of this.*

The pattern is real, Dad. Remember...

Suddenly, his shield blazed with brilliant white light.

No! Don't do this, Molly! He tried to stop it, but this time he lacked the power. The light grew, and the world beneath him faded.

The battle is not in here, Dad. The battle is out there.

And you need to hurry.

Please wait, Garrett sobbed, but it was too late. The light suddenly blazed with the strength of a sun as he regained consciousness. His dream was finished. He had failed.

Chapter Eight

Family Tree

*G*arrett awoke well before eight the next morning. Sunlight peeked between the slits of the heavy curtains that covered the motel window. He shivered and realized that he had left the air conditioning on high. He sat up with a groan, sending a few pages of his research floating to the floor. He had slept above the covers, and now his body was stiff and sore. He massaged his aching knee with a grimace.

The intensity of his dream, like most dreams, was fading. Unlike most dreams, however, the details remained vivid. He remembered everything, from the hellish green light to floating among the stars to diving deep into the sinkhole. He also remembered Molly.

"See the pattern," he muttered. His stomach growled, and he winced. The three lattes were the sum total of his nutritional intake since the previous afternoon. He could feel another headache lurking close by. Before he did anything else, he needed to eat.

The motel boasted a café that featured a small breakfast buffet. Garrett took a quick shower, slipped into fresh clothes, and made his way across the parking lot. The café was a standard motel restaurant, outfitted in muted red, browns and yellows. The smell of scrambled eggs, bacon and pancakes made his stomach growl again. The hostess, an older woman of maybe sixty, led him to a booth. Her name tag read Sarah.

"Coffee?" she asked.

"Just orange juice," he replied with a grimace.

"Help yourself to the buffet," said Sarah. "We've got maple and boysenberry syrup for the pancakes." A memory poked through the layers of time in Garrett's mind. He saw his father, sitting in a roadside café somewhere in Tennessee, pouring boysenberry syrup on a huge stack of pancakes.

He searched and found the proper slot for the memory. He was maybe eight or nine, and they were on vacation. His parents had taken him out of school early, and they had spent a few weeks exploring the mountains. The restaurant had been an early morning discovery, nestled behind a thick tree line somewhere near Gatlinburg. They had almost missed the faded wooden sign announcing that the Mountaineer was open for business. It turned out to be one of those hidden treasures that dotted the winding mountain roads, providing what both his mother and father proclaimed to be the best breakfast ever. It was a good memory, one that had faded thanks to Garrett's ongoing feud with his father. He shook himself back into the present and smiled at Sarah.

"Boysenberry," he said. Sarah disappeared and moments later returned with a small carafe of honest to goodness boysenberry syrup. She set it down, started to leave and then hesitated.

"We're having a get-together tonight over at the armory," she said. "If you're staying the night, you're welcome to come."

"Excuse me?" he asked. Had this woman just asked him on a date?

"It's a combination dance and pot luck dinner," replied Sarah. "The armory gives us a senior citizens discount, and all we ask is that everyone chip in five dollars." She smiled shyly. "You can be my guest if you want." He straightened his shoulders, realizing at that moment that he had been slumping. It was an old man's slump. Between that, his cane, his white hair, and the fact that he was not wearing his ring, it was little wonder that Sarah thought that they were close to the same age. He felt the now familiar bitterness rise in his gullet and forced it down.

"I'm afraid that I'm spoken for," he said, smiling tightly. Sarah raised her eyes, and he could see that she was not buying it…or at least she did not want to buy it. She shrugged and let it drop.

"I leave here at six if you change your mind," she said and started to walk away.

"Do you know the Slave Canal?" He had asked on impulse and was rewarded when she turned and nodded.

"Sure," she said. "It's maybe fifteen or twenty miles from here. Is that where you're headed?"

"I don't know," said Garrett. "Maybe. I hear it's a great place to canoe."

"It is," said Sarah. "Or at least it was when I was there. My husband and I went…well, I guess it's been over twenty years now. We made a day out of it." Her eyes got that far away look that was common to anyone who had stored and catalogued several decades of memories. "We went in April, in the spring. It was so beautiful. Ned was always finding out-of-the-way places like that for us to visit." There was a sad wistfulness in her voice that made Ned's fate obvious.

"How long?" he said softly. She blinked and quickly dabbed the corner of one eye.

"Five years," she said. "Cancer took him."

"I'm sorry," he said, suddenly uncomfortable. She waved his concern away.

"Hey, none of us are young anymore, are we?" she said. "It's life, that's all...just life."

"Just life," muttered Garrett.

"Believe it or not, you're the first man I've asked out since Ned passed," said Sarah. "You can take that as a compliment." That made Garrett smile for real.

"I will," he said. "Thanks."

"Do you know where you're going?" asked Sarah. He started at the question. It hit too close to home. Then he realized that she was still talking about the canal.

"I have no idea," he said, well aware of the double meaning.

"Just take 98 West," she said, "and as soon as you cross the Aucilla, turn north onto the first graded road."

"Graded?" Sarah smiled.

"City boy, eh? It's just a dirt road, although they may have paved it by now. Take it to the end. There used to be a place to rent canoes there. Maybe it's still around."

"I hope so," he said. Another question popped into his mind. "Have you ever heard of anyone calling it Gamble's Run?"

"You meant the canal?" she asked, and Garrett nodded. She gave it some thought. "No, I never heard it called that before, but really, the only time I was ever there was that one time with Ned. Sorry."

"Don't be," said Garrett. "You helped me a lot, and I really appreciate it." Sarah gave him a wistful look and seemed about to say something else, but at that moment a young couple, accompanied by three very noisy children, arrived. She hurried over to greet them. Relieved, Garrett finished his breakfast, left a healthy tip, and went back to his room.

Since the motel did not provide Internet access, he called the front desk to let them know that he would be staying at least one more night. Then he stuffed his research into his satchel along with his laptop and headed back to Starbucks. He winced when he stepped through the main entrance and smelled the brewing coffee, but he managed to hold off the nausea. He ordered another orange juice and managed to snag his booth from the day before. Logging on, he got to work.

This time, he was able to find what he was looking for almost immediately. A brief search led him to a site called Florida Wetland Conservation that kept meticulous records of every sinkhole over the past several years. The instant he called up a map that marked the sinkholes according to their dates, he knew that he had struck pay dirt.

"The big picture," he whispered, staring at the map. The pattern was not easy to see, at least to anyone not looking for it, but it was there. If he traced the sinkholes and cross-referenced them with their dates, he could easily see a long, winding arc. It started maybe forty miles south and gradually worked its way toward the canal. Not surprisingly, his former neighborhood sat well within the arc. Not every sinkhole fit into the pattern, but most did. He could only guess that the holes outside the circle were natural. The ones in the pattern…

"What the hell?" he muttered. "Just what the freaking hell?" The only real conclusion had to be that the sinkholes within that circle were not made by natural causes. He shivered at the implications. *That night was not a natural event*, he thought. *Something attacked us. Did it want Mel and Molly? Was that whole disaster caused for them?* Just thinking about it made him feel sick.

The data only went back five years, but if he took the arc represented by the sinkholes and extrapolated a circle, he could see that it eventually began exactly where it ended…at the Slave Canal. Something was happening deep under the ground, and it had little to do with the drought.

Just how long has this been going on? He pushed the laptop away and pulled out his stack of research. The copies were not double-sided, so he had plenty of scrap paper. He turned one of the sheets over and began writing out the dates on the screen.

Thirty minutes later, he had his answer. If he projected the dates backward, using the length of time between the sinkholes that had occurred over the past five years, the first sinkhole in the pattern would have happened somewhere in the late 1800s. *Definitely John Gamble's era,* he thought. He had not been able to find a date of death for the cotton grower, but it did not matter now. He had unraveled Molly's clue. He had found the pattern.

"So what do I do with it?" he muttered. It was a good question. "Come on, Molly," he said, staring at the map on his screen. "Help me out here." In the booth next to him, a young couple…students, most likely…glanced in his direction, but he ignored them. He knew plenty about the Slave Canal and its creator but was no closer to finding the connection between them and Melody Webb.

"Melinda knows," he said aloud. The couple glanced at him again. He gave them a 'so what' glance, and they quickly looked away. A moment later, they gathered their things and left. *They think I'm a crazy old man*, he thought glumly. He realized that he was slumping again and straightened his shoulders. His back cracked, and he rubbed it absently.

Maybe I am, he thought. *I'm down here chasing what ...ghosts? Demons? I have no idea, and I'm no closer to finding Mel.* He thought of Melinda. He could not believe that she would keep anything from him. She might hate him, but Melody was her only daughter. She would do anything to save her, even if it meant enlisting his help. And yet…

She's hiding something, he thought, *and whatever it is runs deep; maybe so deep that even her sons don't know about it...so deep that she wouldn't even tell me, even if it meant helping Mel.* He shook his head. That made no sense. If she knew something, she would tell him, plain and simple. Unless…

Unless she couldn't tell me...unless something was stopping her from telling me. Somewhere deep in his mind, the synapses were firing. He could feel an answer…or at least a part of an answer…lurking nearby. He drummed his fingers on the table.

"What?" he said aloud. The booths around him were empty, so at least no one was staring. "What are you hiding, Mrs. Chance? What's your connection with John Gamble?"

The instant he said Gamble's name, he saw it. His heart rate doubled, and his breath caught in his throat. *Oh my God,* he thought. *It can't be.* He closed the screen on his laptop. He felt dizzy, as if he was peering over the edge of an impossibly high cliff. *John Gamble. Melinda Chance. That's her maiden name. She took it back when her husband walked out. I must have been blind not to have seen it before.*

He was never good at history, but he did know that slave owners often had sexual relations with their female slaves. These liaisons resulted in biracial children that were almost never acknowledged by their fathers/owners.

"Chance…Gamble," he muttered. "I'll bet that old bastard gave them the name himself, probably as a joke. Either that, or they took it on after they were freed, maybe as a symbol of defiance." Either way, it all added up to one undeniable fact. Melody Webb, formerly Melody Chance, was almost certainly a direct descendant of John Gamble. It was a guess, he knew, but there was one sure way to confirm it.

He did not remember jamming his hand into his pocket and pulling out his cell phone, but he did remember calling up Melinda's number out of his directory. Melinda picked up on the third ring.

"Hello?"

"He's you're, what…great-great-great grandfather?" Melinda drew a harsh breath.

"What did you do to my boy?" she demanded. Her voice shook. Garrett could tell that she was trying to collect herself.

"Why didn't you tell me?" snapped Garrett. "How can Gamble still be around after all this time? What's he got on your family? Why is he tormenting Melody? Is it just because she's his great-whatever-great granddaughter?"

"He doesn't do anything," said Melinda, still speaking about Darrin. "He quit his job, doesn't even leave his house anymore. What did you do to him?"

"No more than what he was trying to do to me," replied Garrett. "He would have put me in the hospital."

"You've got the devil in you, Webb," said Melinda. "And now you put the devil in him."

"Good," hissed Garrett. He could feel the darkness writhing inside him, and a part of him welcomed it. "Now tell me the truth. John Gamble is your ancestor. He is, isn't he?"

"My…leave me alone!"

"No, Melinda, not this time. Tell me the truth."

"I…can't!"

"Tell me!"

"Arvin lit out of here yesterday," said Melinda. "He's coming for you. He knows where you went. Sooner or later he'll find you, and when he does…"

"When he does, I'll give him some of what I gave Darrin," hissed Garrett. The darkness bubbled up. Suddenly, he felt as if it was going to explode out of him. He took a deep breath and forced himself to calm down. "Just tell me what I need to know, Melinda," he said. "Tell me, and I won't bother you again." Melinda was breathing heavily now. Her breath came out in harsh gasps.

"I…can't…" Suddenly, Garrett realized that his initial hunch had been right. Whatever had taken Melody had its claws in Melinda as well. It – *he* - was literally stopping her from answering him. *And that's an answer in itself,* he thought. *Is he doing it now, at this moment, or did he plant some kind of block in her mind?*

His thought process revved into high gear. Melinda might be prevented from telling him about her family tree, but maybe he could come at it from another angle.

"Your family came from Florida, didn't they? They came from this area, in fact."

"Y…yes," said Melinda. She was panting now, and although he could not see her, Garrett was certain that she was sweating.

"Your line runs deep here," said Garrett. "Generations, I would guess."

"Many…generations," said Melinda. "All the way back before the war."

"The Civil War," said Garrett.

"Y…yes," replied Melinda. She seemed barely able to speak, but to her credit, she was trying. Garrett kept going.

"Your people were slaves here," he said. "They worked the cotton plantations."

"That…and other things," said Melinda. *Bingo*, thought Garrett. Despite their mutual loathing, he felt a grudging respect for Melody's mother. The same unforgiving determination that had raised three children as a single mother was now working for him. Melinda was fighting tooth and nail whatever hold Gamble had on her. For the moment, at least, she was winning.

"That's where it started," said Garrett. "With the 'other things'."

"Ye…yes." Garrett thought furiously. What did he need to know that he had not already figured out? An idea flared in his mind.

"Were you an only child?" he asked.

"I…had a sister," said Melinda. "She died years ago."

"How?"

"She…I…can't…"

"Never mind," said Garrett. The answer was obvious. Gamble had taken her sister, just as he had taken Melody.

"And your mother?" he asked. "What about her family?"

"My aunt died when she was twenty-five," said Melinda. Was that approval in her voice? Garrett couldn't have cared less. The last thing he needed was Melinda's approval.

"You moved to Kentucky not long after Melody was born," he said. "You moved to protect her. You tried to get away." Melinda's only answer was her heavy breathing. *Too direct,* he thought. He tried again.

"It doesn't make sense," he said. "Why did Melody agree to go back to Florida with me? Why did she encourage me to take that job? Why…oh dear God!" The implication hit him full force. His throat went try, and he gulped down a few mouthfuls of orange juice. "Was I manipulated?" he asked. "My job, our move, all of it; was it to get Melody down here?" The idea was absurd, but the instant he said it, it *felt* right.

"The waters…run…deep," gasped Melinda. "They…reach out to everyone, especially to those whose family lines go…way back."

"What? What's that mean, Melinda?" The only answer Melinda gave him…*could* give him…was her now desperate panting. *The waters,* he thought. *Gamble? Just how much influence does he have here?*

His former boss, Anthony Tope, used to boast about how his family had lived in the area for generations. Garrett flashed back to how he had landed the Florida job. A corporate headhunter had contacted him. The offer had been more than generous, and Melody had encouraged him to take it. The nausea he had been fighting since he arrived at Starbucks made a curtain call. Now he was the one taking deep breaths, trying to prevent Sarah's pancakes from splashing all over the table. Had John Gamble somehow influenced Anthony to hire him?

"The waters run deep," he muttered.

"Yes," breathed Melinda.

"But why did Melody..." and the answer hit him. "She didn't know," he said.

"N...no."

"And you couldn't tell her," said Garrett. "You were *stopped* from telling her." Silence. "He had his finger on her," he said. "He probably had his finger on her from birth." More silence. His questions were too direct now, but he no longer cared.

"How do I stop him, Melinda? *Can* I stop him?"

"You...you've got to try!"

"How? How do I fight him? How do I get Melody back?"

"I DON"T KNOW," screamed Melinda. "I DON'T...aaaiiiiieeee!" Garrett jerked the phone away from his head. Melinda's scream had nearly shattered his eardrum. He held it back to his ear, but the connection was broken.

"No," he hissed, thumbing the redial button, but before the call could go through, the phone's screen flashed once, then twice. "What the..." The screen went dark. Garrett hit the 'ON' button over and over again, but nothing happened. His phone was dead. He shook it and tried again, but nothing happened.

"Damn you," he growled, staring at the phone. The screen flared to life, only now it glowed with a disease ridden green light that he knew all too well. In the midst of that light, two black words appeared.

STAY AWAY

Seconds later, the glow faded. Garrett tapped a few buttons, but the phone was dead, this time for good. With a snarl, he stuffed his computer and papers into his satchel and headed for the exit. On the way out, he threw his phone into the trash.

Despite the encounter, a glimmer of hope now shone through the darkness in his soul. Melinda had confirmed his guess about Melody's lineage, and the incident with the phone suggested that he might be heading in the right direction.

Unfortunately, time was still against him. Both Melinda's sister and aunt had been taken by the creature they called John Gamble. Now it had Melody, and if he could not act fast enough, Gamble would destroy her as well.

He drove away from the Starbucks, heading back to his motel. There was no more time for research, no more time to try to piece together the mystery that was Gamble's Run. He was going to have to make the journey to the Slave Canal and pierce whatever mysteries awaited him within its depths.

Chapter 9

Sam's Bait and Tackle

*G*arrett found a small sporting goods store where he purchased a knapsack and a pair of sturdy hiking boots. To this he added several foil bags of dried food and a large thermos. The clerk rang up his sale with a cocked eyebrow, taking in his frail appearance. Garrett swallowed his pride and allowed the clerk to carry his purchases to his car. By the time he left the store, it was late in the afternoon. He decided to spend one more night at the motel.

He set out the next morning at daybreak. Less than an hour later, he crossed the Aucilla River. He found the dirt road, although it was little more than a wilderness trail, barely wide enough for a single car. There was a narrow grass strip on the right. Beyond that was a thick line of trees and brush. On the other side, the tree line bordered the edge of the road. If he met an oncoming car, there would be just enough room to ease over into the grass and inch past. Judging from the weeds growing in the center, it was not heavily traveled.

He swung onto the road and started forward, but almost immediately he had to stop. The drought from the previous year had returned in force. Dirt from the surface flew up in every direction, completely obscuring his vision. He skidded to a halt, waiting for the dust cloud to dissipate. After several minutes, he was able to see again. He started forward, inching along so as not to create another cloud.

There were no signs along the way, and as he crept deeper into the country, he began to get worried. If this barely navigable road suddenly ended, would there be enough room to turn around? It was a very real concern. Without his cell phone, he was effectively cut off from the rest of the world. If his car got stuck, he would have to hoof it back to civilization, and with his bad knee, his chances of success were questionable at best.

He bounced along, aware that he was probably doing serious harm to the suspension of his car. There were deep potholes, and more than once he heard the underside of his car scrape against the loose dirt.

Thirty minutes later, the road emptied out into a small clearing. He breathed a sigh of relief when he saw a wooden shack about the size and shape of a convenience store. It sat at the far end of the clearing, maybe twenty yards away. Two vehicles were parked in front…a fairly new white Chevrolet SUV and an older, battered red Ford pickup truck. Both were covered with dust.

The paint on the building was cracked and faded and might have once been yellow. Two feet tall letters running across the top of the structure told him that he had just found Sam's Bait and Tackle Shop. A sign next to a battered screened door announced that the place was open, although given its remote location, Garrett could not figure out how the place stayed in business.

Underneath the first sign was another one with big red letters that read 'Canoe Rentals Here!' Next to the door was a large picture window. Painted on it was an impressive fish…Garrett had no idea what kind…that was about to bite into a hook disguised as a smaller fish.

"It's a start," he muttered as he eased his car up to the shop. He shut off the engine, grabbed his cane and got out, grimacing as the pain in his knee flared. Scenes from a dozen horror movies…the kind that featured a masked killer slicing his way through a swarm of screaming teenagers at summer camp…flashed through his mind. He shoved them aside and headed toward the entrance. The back of his neck itched, and he had to resist the urge to hunch his shoulders. He felt as if someone was staring at him from beyond the tree line. He stopped and turned, scanning the forest. No one was in sight. Of course, they could be easily hidden in the dense brush. He stared at the forest a moment longer, trying to pinpoint the source of his unease. Finally, it hit him.

As Sarah had deduced, Garrett was a city boy at heart. The everyday background noises common to a large group of people living in relatively close quarters were deeply ingrained into his psyche. Now, those noises were missing. There were no cars buzzing by on a nearby highway, and no one was playing a stereo too loud. Instead, a single bird was chirping in the distance. A gentle breeze rustled the leaves of the nearby trees. There was nothing else.

I guess that appeals to some people, he thought as he started toward the door again, *But I don't think I like it.*

He shrugged off his unease, pushed the door open and stepped inside.

A half-dozen overlapping odors hit him as he entered. The most powerful was the somewhat nauseating smell of live bait. He could see several waist high metal troughs off to his left against the wall, where the offered bait…most probably minnows or some other breed of tiny fish…was kept. A low hum, accompanied by the sound of bubbling water, told him that the filtration system was working. He wondered where the power was coming from, as there were no visible power lines outside. *Probably a generator out back*, he thought.

Two large fans, hanging from the ceiling, rotated slowly, moving the warm air back and forth. The morning was still young, but the temperature outside was well into the eighties. The store had no air conditioning, but it was marginally cooler inside, thanks to the fans. Garrett felt a tiny drip of sweat trickle down his forehead and wiped it away absently.

To his right, at least two dozen fishing rods were lined up on a high shelf, leaning against the wall like tired soldiers. They came in all shapes, sizes and colors. A few even had reels attached. In the center of the store were two rows of chest-high free standing shelves that held assorted tackle, lures and other fishing paraphernalia. Immediately to his left was a low shelf that ran under the front window. It held canteens, knapsacks and other camping supplies.

Directly in front of him, about fifteen feet away, was a waist high glass counter. Displayed within it were fishing reels, probably of the more expensive sort. A cash register sat at one end of the counter. Behind that was a refrigeration unit, placed against the back wall.

Through the frosted glass doors he could see sodas, bottled water and beer. The floor was made of wood, darkened with age, which creaked with every step.

Garrett stepped all the way inside. The screen door swung gently shut behind him. The place was empty. There was no buzzer or bell hanging over the door to warn whoever might be on duty that a potential customer had arrived.

"Hello," he called out…not very loud. There was a sleepy silence about the place that seemed to discourage unnecessary noise. The only sound was coming from the bait tanks and the fans. He stepped across the shop to the glass case. To the right of the refrigeration unit was an open door that led to what was probably a small stock room. He could see daylight streaming through and guessed that the back door was standing open. "Hello," he called out, just a little louder.

"Just a second," came a male voice from beyond the door. Garrett jumped. Although he knew that someone was nearby…the dusty truck and SUV had told him as much…he had not really expected an answer. He heard a thump, as if something heavy had fallen, followed by muted cursing. Then a shadow fell across the door behind a counter. A second later, the owner of the voice stepped through.

Garrett blinked. He had been expecting a grizzled, older outdoorsy type…the kind of man who loved to entertain his guests around a campfire with ghost stories or who chopped up unsuspecting teenagers. Instead, he found himself face to face with a younger man, somewhere in his mid-thirties. His dark hair was cut short, and his bright blue eyes accented his broad, friendly face. He was slouching, but Garrett guessed that if he stood up straight, he might top six feet with an inch or two left over. He was wearing jeans and a plain white T-shirt, but Garrett could have just as easily placed him in a conservative business suit.

"Hey there," he called out in a cheery voice. "How can I help you?"

"Are you Sam?" Garrett asked. The man shook his head.

"Nope," he said. "Sam was my grandfather. He started this business over eighty years ago, and as you can see, I have taken it and molded it into the financial empire that it is today." Garrett chuckled at the joke. Somewhere in the back of his mind, a masked killer vanished in a puff of smoke. The man held out a hand. "I'm Kyle Masterson," he said, "owner, clerk, stock boy and all around great guy." Garrett took the proffered hand and shook it. Kyle's grip was firm and strong.

"Garrett," he said. "Garrett Webb."

"Good to meet you," said Kyle. "So how can I help you on this fine day?"

"I want to rent a canoe," said Garrett. "They're available here, right?" For the first time, Kyle frowned. He glanced down at Garrett's knee and cane.

"Sure," he said. "Mind if I ask where you want to go?"

"The Slave Canal," said Garrett. "Someone told me that this where I start." Kyle nodded.

"It is," said Kyle. "One of a few places in the area, at least. There's Dusty's…that's a few miles north of here, and Sally Blaine's place down closer to Nutall Rise, but yeah, you can get to the canal from here."

"That's where I want to go," said Garrett.

"Alone?" asked Kyle. Garrett nodded.

"Is that a problem?" he asked. Kyle hesitated. Garrett could see that he did not want to offend a potential customer.

"It is, actually," he said after a moment. "You take the Wacissia…that's a few miles from here…and it will lead you straight to the canal. Once you get in, you can follow it all the way to Nutall Rise. That's where most folk end their trip."

"So what's the problem?"

"Well," said Kyle, "the current's not all that bad, and the river flows in the direction of the canal. The problem is getting back. Five miles against even a weak current can beat a strong man." He glanced pointedly at Garrett's cane, his meaning obvious. Garrett said nothing. "Most of the day trippers come in groups and park at least one car at Nutall Rise," continued Kyle. "I leave a couple of trailers there so they can bring the canoes back. Either that or I charge them extra to go pick them up."

"What happens if they decide to steal them?" asked Garrett. Kyle chuckled at the question.

"The deposit," he said. "It's more than the canoe is worth, so if they want it, they can have it." Garrett nodded.

"I'd be willing to pay you extra to come and get me along with the canoe," he said. Kyle shook his head.

"You ever been through the canal before?" he asked.

"First time," said Garrett.

"Then you can't go alone," said Kyle. His tone allowed for no argument. "Even folks who have made the trip sometimes have a problem finding the entrance, and if you miss it, you'll end up in the Warriors. That's…"

"I've read about the Warriors," said Garrett.

"Then you know that they're a maze," said Kyle. "And they're dangerous. They're not all that deep, but they come equipped with gators and assorted snakes, a few of which are poisonous. Add to that the fact that it's easy to get lost in there, and you could have a real problem. That happened to a young couple just last year. It took a police helicopter over an hour to find them. I had to go get them myself." He smiled at the memory. "That was one humiliated couple." He looked at Garrett's cane again. "I'm sorry, Mr. Webb, but I just can't rent you a canoe. To be blunt, you don't look up to the trip. If anything happened to you, I'd be responsible." Garrett's mind shifted into high gear.

I'll buy a canoe, he thought. *According to the maps, there's a lot of open country around here. I'll find a place to launch and get to the canal, one way or the other.*

"...if you're willing, that is. How about it?" Garrett blinked and realized that Kyle had not stopped talking.

"Sorry," he said, embarrassed. "My mind was wandering." Kyle pursed his lips, and Garrett was suddenly certain that the store owner knew exactly what he had been considering.

"I said that I just rented a couple of canoes to some day trippers. They're regular customers...come up here once or twice a year, so they know what they're doing. They left here on foot about ten minutes ago. It's about a mile hike to the shed where I keep the canoes, so I doubt that they're at the river yet. The path winds something fierce. If you want to see if you can tag along with them, we can take my truck. We'll swing around on the road and meet them at the river. You can ask them yourself. How about that?" Garrett took a few seconds to mull it over and then nodded.

"I'd really appreciate it," he said. He meant it. If finding the entrance to the canal was as difficult as Kyle said, he was going to need the help. Kyle smiled.

"Come on, then," he said, heading toward the screen door. "We'll have to hurry, but I think we can catch them." He led the way outside to the pickup.

"Why is this place so far away from the river...or the main road, for that matter?" Garrett asked as he retrieved his knapsack from the trunk of his car.

"My grandfather used to own all of the land between here and the river," replied Kyle, opening the rider's door of his truck. "But he had to sell it to pay some debts. It belongs to the state of Florida now. Granddad built this place not long after he sold the land, and my dad and I managed to make it work...local customers mostly." He took Garrett's knapsack and threw it into the bed of the truck. He waited as Garrett climbed into the cab. Then he swung his door shut, trotted over to the other side and got in behind the wheel. "So why the canal?" he said, starting the engine, "if you don't mind my asking, that is."

Actually, I mind a lot, thought Garrett.

"I'm a Civil War buff," he said aloud. "I didn't even know it existed until I ran across a reference to it while I was doing some other research. It's not really well known." Kyle nodded. He turned the truck around. A moment later, they were bouncing along the same dirt road Garrett had followed earlier. He had not noticed that it continued on the far side of the clearing. The dust swirled around them, but Kyle ignored it. The lack of visibility made Garrett nervous, but he decided to trust that his guide knew what he was doing.

"We like it like that," Kyle said. "The lack of attention, I mean. We don't mind a few day trippers coming through…most of them are nice enough. Once or twice a year, an expedition from the university comes by. They're good people, and they don't make a fuss. Sometimes they find some interesting things from the people who lived here a long time ago."

"That would be the Paleo," said Garrett. Kyle glanced at him, his eyebrows raised in surprise.

"You *have* done your research," he said. "Yeah, them. They dive the canal….the scientists I mean, not the Paleo." Garrett smiled.

"I thought it was only a few feet deep?" he said.

"Most of it is," said Kyle, "But the water has worn it deeper in a few places. Anyway, the scientists dive the canal and excavate the mounds."

"Mounds?"

"There's a few of them in the vicinity of the canal, although they predate it. One of the professors told me that they were made maybe thousands of years ago. He said that there wasn't even a river here then."

"Only springs and sinkholes," muttered Garrett. Kyle gave him a sideways glance.

"Yeah," he said. "The river came later, and of course the canal itself is only a hundred and fifty or so years old." Garrett nodded. "Anyway," continued Kyle, "we get some fishermen, a few day trippers, and the occasional scientist. Not many others. Like I said, we like it like that. We really don't want our canal turned into some kind of half-assed shrine."

"Our canal?" asked Garrett. Kyle nodded firmly.

"*Our* canal," he said. "We might not own the property, but it's ours."

"You mean the locals?"

"The natives," corrected Kyle, "the folks who have lived here for generations. You'd be surprised how many descendants of the slaves who dug the canal still live around here."

"Really," said Garrett, fascinated.

"Oh yeah," said Kyle. "There's the Foreman family near Nutall Rise. The Coates family lives a little further south. A few others are scattered about the area. They're all good friends." His tone changed slightly when he said friends, and Garrett picked up on it immediately. He had lived with racism from both his and Melody's family long enough to recognize it, even in its subtlest form. The unease he had felt outside of Kyle's store returned.

"As for the rest of us," Kyle continued. "Well, the Gamble family died out a generation ago. My family runs back to before the Civil War. A lot of families around here can trace their line back that far…some even further." Garrett started to ask Kyle if he knew the Chance family but bit the question back at the last second. Kyle's racism aside, he did not want to draw attention to the real reason for his visit.

"I read that someone in the government tried to rename it a while back," he said instead. Kyle snorted.

"Tried…and failed. Cotton Run Canal, my ass. It's the Slave Canal. It's going to stay the Slave Canal, no matter what some low level bureaucrat says."

"Have you ever heard it called Gamble's Run?" It felt like a safe enough question, but the instant he asked it, Garrett knew that he had made a serious mistake. He looked at Kyle, expecting nothing more than a mild denial. Instead, Kyle tightened his grip on the steering wheel. His eyes narrowed, and he glanced sideways at Garrett.